SAY YOU'LL LOVE ME

AN UNEXPECTED SUITOR NOVEL

Say You'll Love Me

An Unexpected Suitor Novel

ALLY BROADFIELD

Entangled Publishing, LLC
2614 South Timberline Road
Suite 109
Fort Collins, CO 80525
Visit our website at www.entangledpublishing.com.

Scandalous is an imprint of Entangled Publishing, LLC.

Edited by Robin Haseltine
Cover Design by LJ Anderson
Cover Art by Period Images

ISBN 978-1-943892-87-7

Manufactured in the United States of America

First Edition October 2015

Scandalous
an Entangled imprint

To everyone who believes in happily ever after.

Chapter One

Despite Lord Wrexham's ballroom being dimly lit, with widely spaced chandeliers and burgundy silk wallpaper that did nothing to dispel the dreary atmosphere, Lady Abigail Hurst would not allow it to dampen her spirits. This was her night. At long last, she was attending her own betrothal ball.

She drew in a prolonged breath before cementing a smile on her face and striding forward to greet her soon-to-be mother-in-law.

"My lady, it is a pleasure to see you again." She executed a low curtsy. Though she had known Lady Wrexham for most of her life, as her father's estate shared a border with Lord Wrexham's country property, this was their first encounter since Abigail had officially become betrothed to her son, Robert, who currently held the title of Viscount Hinsdale.

Lady Wrexham's eyes traveled up to the top of Abigail's

head and all the way back down to her toes which, thankfully, were doubly concealed by her slippers and ball gown. She resisted the urge to reach up and check her hair for loose tendrils. The stern expression on Lady Wrexham's face didn't waver, and Abigail was left feeling she had failed the first of many tests in her near future. She had never been particularly comfortable in public, and Lady Wrexham was hardly bolstering her confidence.

"You are shorter than I remember," Lady Wrexham said.

Abigail's mother widened her eyes, indicating she should reply, but honestly, how was she to respond to that? She was fairly certain she hadn't been shrinking.

"I suppose you'll do." Lady Wrexham waved a loose hand at Abigail. "Your father is tall enough, and you are passably attractive. The men have made their decision and we can't expect any better from them."

"Thank you, my lady." Abigail was relieved that Lady Wrexham's expectations of her were so low. Hopefully, her son would have higher standards. Her stomach fluttered at the thought of seeing Robert. Despite the long-standing expectations of their parents that they would one day marry, Robert had been away traveling on the continent for so long that she had begun to doubt this day would ever come; but it was here now and she intended to enjoy it. Robert had been the epitome of courtesy and charm since his return, and she found herself wishing they had already wed.

"Go along now," Lady Wrexham said. "You've made an excellent match with my son and you must accept your congratulations from our guests."

Pleased to be given her freedom, Abigail sought the retiring room before the dancing began. She followed the edge of the ballroom, using the wall to help her discern an exit amidst the shadowed edges of the room. After entering the first corridor she came to, she slowed and took in her surroundings. Surely Lady Wrexham would not expect her guests to traverse an unlit path. She must have stumbled upon a servant's passage of some sort. As she turned to go back to the ballroom, she discerned the outline of a man and woman in close proximity farther down the corridor.

"My lord, we will have to continue this conversation later. I must return before Lady Jane notes my absence," said a feminine voice.

The lord in question's back was turned toward Abigail. He wore evening clothes, clearly intending to attend the ball, but he had the maid pushed up against the wall, her skirts lifted, his hand between…oh my.

"My lord, please," the maid begged. The flicker of the candle in the wall sconce illuminated the tears on her cheek.

He dropped her skirts abruptly. "I will seek you out after the ball."

Abigail stiffened, horrified at the sound of her intended's voice. She backed away carefully, her slippers blessedly silent against the wood floor, dread heavy upon her. The retiring room forgotten, she whirled and scurried toward the ballroom, seeking escape to anywhere else before he noticed her.

Moving quickly, she slipped into another empty corridor and leaned against the wall. Though she was aware that some men consorted with women who were not their wives, she had not expected Robert to be one of them. And with his younger sister's lady's maid, at that. The maid had said that Lady Jane would note her absence.

Abigail forced herself to inhale and exhale slowly, willing her heart to stop racing. After a few more deep breaths, her heart ceased its frantic beating and her mind cleared. She must accept that he had been carrying on with the maid prior to their formal betrothal, but surely he would stop now that they were finally to be married and he would no longer live in this house. For now, she would focus on the ball and not allow what might be a small indiscretion to taint what ought to be the happiest night of her life. After all, this was Robert. He had played lawn bowls with her and taught her how to skip stones and drive a curricle.

Abigail lifted her chin and reentered the ballroom. A scan of the room revealed Lady Georgiana Townsend in conversation with her elder sister. She let out a pent up breath and moved toward them.

"Lady Varnham, Lady Georgiana, how lovely to see you." Though they were on a first name basis, Abigail used their proper titles lest Lady Wrexham overhear their conversation and find fault with their familiarity.

"Abigail," Henrietta said, dispensing with formality, "I believe congratulations are in order. I wish you joy and happiness in your alliance."

Abigail took her proffered hand. "Thank you, Henrietta." Though it wasn't well known among the *ton*, Henrietta had narrowly survived a disastrous, but thankfully brief, marriage to an abusive husband.

Georgiana was the first person Abigail had told about her betrothal, so there was no need for felicitations from her. Robert's association with the maid still weighed heavily on her mind, and if they were anywhere else, Abigail would have told her what she just witnessed.

"Is there something amiss?" Georgiana asked. "You are pale."

As if her will meant nothing, the words slipped out unbidden. "I couldn't see well enough to tell who it was, but I witnessed a nobleman making free with one of the maids in the corridor." Abigail lowered her voice and moved closer. "The maid begged him to stop, and he reluctantly dropped her skirt, but told her to expect him after the ball."

"Oh, my," Georgiana said.

Henrietta's eyes were wide with fright. Abigail chastised herself. It was unkind of her to mention the incident in front of Henrietta. She ought not to have said anything at all. "I will speak with Robert about it and make sure he puts a stop to it." The twisted irony of her words robbed her of breath for a moment. She patted Henrietta's hand.

Henrietta and Georgiana's older brother, Edmund Townsend, the Marquess of Longcroft, joined them.

He bowed. "Lady Abigail, I understand congratulations are in order."

"Yes, thank you, my lord." Abigail wasn't sure what to think of Lord Longcroft. She was surprised to see him here since she knew from her friend's frequent complaints that he loathed attending social events, and most especially balls. But with responsibility for six unwed sisters, he could not withdraw from society all together.

The string quartet took position across the room, signaling that the dancing would soon begin.

"Lady Abigail, would you care to join me for the first dance?" Lord Longcroft asked.

Handsome in an unconventional sort of way, he was wider through the shoulders than Robert, with hair the color of polished mahogany that was longer than the current fashion. Georgiana had joked that he was so engrossed in his studies of science and mathematics that he sometimes forgot to tend to mundane things like having his hair trimmed.

"I thank you, my lord, but I have promised the first dance to my intended."

"Yes, yes, of course. How silly of me." He gave her a crooked grin.

Just then, Robert entered their circle. "Lady Varnham, Lady Georgiana." Robert bowed over each of their hands before turning to nod to their brother. "Longcroft."

Robert's warm hand pressed against her back. "Shall we?"

Her stomach fluttered with a peculiar mix of excitement and dread. "By all means." Everyone in the ballroom was focused on them as he led her to the center of the floor to dance the minuet. Lady Wrexham was very traditional and wouldn't dream of starting a ball with any other dance.

Robert smiled and stroked the inside of her wrist in a soothing circular pattern as they allowed the other dancers time to take their places. Perhaps Abigail was mistaken, and the incident she'd witnessed with the maid wasn't as horrible as she'd thought. Surely the maid was crying because she didn't want Lady Jane to scold her, and not because she was afraid of Robert. Abigail would give her betrothed the benefit of the doubt and stop behaving like a silly girl instead of a mature woman who would soon be married. She squared her shoulders, determined that no one detect her inner turmoil.

Despite her central location, Abigail was unable to locate Georgiana among the dancers. Even with the aid of the wall sconces, the light was too dim for her to make out the faces of any of the guests at the edges of the ballroom. When she became mistress of this house, she would immediately have the room painted in bright tones and have more chandeliers installed in the ballroom.

The notes of the minuet surrounded them and they began to move. Normally when she danced, she would hold a conversation with her partner as the movements of the dance allowed, but Robert was strangely silent, distracted even. They had known each other for as long as she could remember. As children, they had explored Yorkshire together. She had always been the first person he visited during his school holidays. Nothing had ever been awkward between them until tonight.

She accepted the fact that she wasn't a great beauty who inspired sonnets or other such attention, and Robert had never been anything but polite and kind to her. If her stomach quivered slightly when thoughts of him consorting with his sister's maid entered her mind, well surely that was natural for a young, inexperienced girl. Her social circle was quite limited, and aside from Henrietta, she wasn't acquainted with anyone who had married yet. It would have been helpful to find that other women grappled with the same feelings as their weddings rapidly approached, but she knew not whom to ask.

"The ballroom looks lovely this evening," she said to break the silence.

Robert nodded.

"Do you know who created the flower arrangements?" In truth, they weren't very impressive, but at least a question required a response.

"No. You'll have to ask Mother." He kept looking toward

the entrance as if anticipating someone's arrival.

To distract herself from obsessing over the maid, she reverted to her favorite activity. In her mind, she redesigned the gowns of the ladies around her. Mama had once commented that had she been born to a different family, she would have made an excellent modiste.

After vowing not to allow anyone to convince her to use Lady Wrexham's seamstress, she began with Robert's mother because she was clearly in need of the most help. Instead of the pale peach color, which in Abigail's opinion was inappropriate for a woman of Lady Wrexham's age—not to mention how unpleasantly it blended with her mottled complexion—she would use a deep blue to bring out the color in her eyes. A lower neckline, enhanced with tiny seed pearls embroidered in a circular pattern on the bodice and above the hem. Oh, and a sash of the finest—

"Abigail? You seem worlds away."

Now he deigned to speak with her, just as she was about to decide on the *piece de resistance* of his mother's gown. "My apologies," she said as she moved away from him. When they came back together, she said, "Was there something you wanted to ask?"

"Not particularly." He laughed as they spun around. "You were so intent, I merely wished to know what was occupying your mind."

This was a good sign indeed. "Well, if you must know, I was thinking about ways to improve your mother's gown."

His eyes narrowed immediately, and she regretted her sudden impulse to share her innermost thoughts with him.

"That is not only an insult to her modiste, but my mother as well," he said stiffly.

She wished she could melt through the floorboards. It seemed nothing would go her way this evening. "I meant no insult. I merely thought that a more vibrant color would emphasize her beautiful eyes."

"What a strange way for a lady to occupy herself. I shall have to come up with more productive activities to occupy your mind." His eyes sparkled as his lips curved into a smile. "I must agree that she does rather resemble a pumpkin in that gown."

And just like that, he dispelled her worry. He was still the Robert she had known. She simply needed to spend more time with him, get to know him more intimately, as she had when they were younger, and then she would be able to interpret his words and moods more accurately. It was unreasonable for her to expect him to still be the boy that she had once known so well. The eldest of her brothers was eight years her junior, so she had very little experience interacting with men. Except for Papa, of course, but that was very different.

They finished the set, and Robert guided her back to her mother. He kissed her hand. "Save the first waltz for me."

"Of course." She returned his smile and tracked him as he strode down a corridor leading away from the ballroom. Thankfully, it was not the same passage where she had happened upon him earlier. After accepting a glass of champagne from a passing footman, she sipped it the way her governess had taught her rather than gulping it down, as she would have preferred, to dampen her nerves.

After receiving congratulations from several people and securing three offers to dance, Robert still had not returned to the ballroom. With each passing moment, the weight of her doubts about Robert pressed harder upon her, making it difficult to breathe deeply.

The first waltz was set to start as soon as the current set ended. It was odd that her betrothed would seclude himself in the card room when this ball was being held in their honor. Perhaps he was similarly weighted down by guilt over his reprehensible behavior, as well he should be. Papa entered the ballroom and approached. Maybe he would know Robert's whereabouts.

"Are you enjoying yourself, my dear?" he asked.

She continued to skim the perimeter of the ballroom. "Yes, of course, but I'm wondering why Robert is spending so long sequestered in the card room."

His brows drew together. "Robert isn't in the card room."

Her pulse jumped a notch. Where could he be? "He asked me to save the first waltz for him, but he seems to have disappeared."

He patted her hand. "No need to worry. I'll go speak with Lord Wrexham and see if we can hunt your young man down."

Papa was not fond of dancing, or society in general, so he was likely grateful for the excuse to exit the ballroom. He preferred to spend his time at his club, and only occasionally accompanied Abigail and her mother to society functions when Mama insisted.

"Lady Abigail." The deep tones of Lord Longcroft reached her like a caress to her frazzled nerves. "Would you care to dance?"

She placed her hand in his. "I would be honored." Abigail hoped Robert wouldn't be angry with her if he suddenly returned and found her waltzing with Lord Longcroft, but

Robert had certainly been less attentive than he ought to have been, considering this was their betrothal ball, and she so loved to waltz.

He led her onto the floor, and as they took their positions, she caught Georgiana smiling from the edge of the ballroom. She must have noted Abigail's distress and sent her brother to occupy her. There was no other reason he would choose to dance with her. Though Abigail spent a fair amount of time at his home, she saw him only rarely when she visited with Georgiana, as he was generally sequestered in his library working on some project or another.

Lord Longcroft wore a perplexed expression. "So tell me, since I'm never quite sure, what is one meant to discuss while dancing?"

She couldn't quash the smile that curved her lips at his guileless question. Warmth emanated from his body, enveloping her in a safe cocoon, and she relaxed for the first time since the ball had begun. "Perhaps the weather, the current state of the roads, or a compliment on the decorations."

"So the more monotonous, the better?" he asked.

Another involuntary smile overcame her. "Precisely. Or, awkward silence is always an option."

His eyes widened. "I'm afraid awkward silence causes me to start performing calculations in my mind, guaranteeing that the conversation will be lacking for the remainder of the set."

She hadn't realized how much taller he was than Robert. She had to tilt her head back to meet his deep brown eyes, the color of roasted chestnuts. "What sort of calculations do you perform?"

"It depends on what I'm working on at the time. Tonight,

for example, since I'm focused on updating our greenhouse, I would attempt to calculate how much wind pressure a pane of glass can sustain." He glanced over his shoulder, guiding her to avoid a collision with another couple.

She frowned. "Oh, dear. I'm afraid I would need paper to work out calculations of that nature."

"Most people do. I just happen to perform so many more calculations than anyone else would that I've developed an aptitude for solving them in my head." One corner of his mouth turned up in a wry smile.

"An impressive feat indeed." She raised her brows. "But why not just test the glass instead?"

He nodded to a passing acquaintance. "Some might go that route, but the tax on glass is so deuced high right now that I find taking the time to perform the calculations to be the most logical step."

She bit her lip to keep from smiling again, afraid she looked like a raving lunatic to anyone watching. "Rightly so." Their conversation trailed off for a moment as she perused the ballroom. There was still no sign of Robert. She had half expected him to interrupt their dance.

She turned back toward Lord Longcroft. Georgiana had claimed that he avoided society because he had six sisters to marry off, but upon further examination, Abigail determined that it was more likely to avoid being overrun with female admirers. Underneath his shaggy exterior, he was quite handsome and almost entirely without artifice. Not to mention being wealthy and a marquess. He would be much sought after on the marriage mart if word were to get out that he was seeking a wife.

She decided that a mutual confession was in order.

"When left to my own devices, I redesign the gowns of the ladies."

He flicked his head to the side to move the hair from his eyes. "Indeed. What sort of changes do you imagine?"

"Well, it depends on the lady and the gown, of course."

He nodded sagely.

"But usually a more appropriate color, some embellishments like a sash or beading, and a lower or higher neckline."

"What would you recommend for Lady Needler?" He discreetly tilted his head toward the lady in question.

It was an interesting choice, and she suddenly wondered what he thought of the lady in question, and whether he found her attractive or gauche. "First, I would change the color from yellow, which makes her skin look wan, to pink to bring out her natural skin tone. Then, in this case, I would raise the neckline." Which, in Abigail's opinion, was scandalously low on her ample bosom.

"A wise decision, that." He leaned closer and spoke into her ear, his heated breath sending shivers up her neck. "Imagine if they were dancing a Scotch Reel. Her partner would have to worry about one of those beasts breaking free and pummeling him."

Abigail responded with a very unladylike snort in her attempt not to laugh out loud. She should be scandalized by his blunt speech, but it was so exactly in line with what she had been thinking she couldn't bear to correct him.

Lord Longcroft was contrite. "My apologies, Lady Abigail. I should never have said that to you." He looked down for a moment. "It's just that I'm used to speaking frankly with my sisters, and I'm out in society so infrequently that I forgot for a moment to whom I was speaking. I hope I did not offend you."

"It's quite all right. I haven't been this entertained in a very long time." She leaned a bit closer to him. "And I couldn't agree more."

The music ended and Robert and her father entered the ballroom while Lord Longcroft walked her back to Mama. She had been so absorbed in their conversation that she had forgotten for a moment about Robert's strange absence.

Her father's face was grave.

Lord Longcroft took his leave, then Robert clasped her hand and smoothed the top with his thumb. His eyes were wide and unfocused. "My apologies for leaving you on your own, my dear. Though there is nothing for you to be concerned about, I'm afraid my sister's maid has disappeared under questionable circumstances."

Chapter Two

Abigail slept fitfully. The image of Robert with his sister's maid invaded her dreams and woke her repeatedly throughout the night. She had half hoped it had all been a bad dream. And yet, the incident last night had punctuated the fact that she was not in love with Robert. Even if she hadn't witnessed him with the maid, he did not fulfill her vision of true love. At one time she had thought herself in love with him, but they had changed and grown apart, and he was not the man of her dreams.

Sunlight cascaded through the space between her curtains and she sat up and rubbed Baxter's ears. Her restlessness had kept him awake all night as well, and based on the position of the sun, it was now afternoon.

"I'm sorry, dearest. You're probably as exhausted as I am." She kissed the top of his head. "The difference is that you can sleep whenever you please, whereas I will need to remain awake for the larger part of the day." Baxter was a foxhound bred from her father's pack. As a small puppy, he had been injured by an older dog, and she narrowly rescued him from being drowned by the hound keeper. He had been by her side ever since.

Her maid, Judith, bustled in and began preparations for Abigail's bath. Once she was bathed and dressed, Abigail went to the parlor to check the morning paper for information about the missing maid. Jane would be distraught if the girl had not yet been found. She was several years younger than Abigail and was like a sister to her, since she had only brothers.

Mama glanced up as she entered the room and patted the cushion next to her. "Come and sit with me."

The Morning Post sat on the table in front of her. She reached for the paper while fear and curiosity surged through her in equal measure.

"Don't be hasty." Mama took the paper from her hand and laid it back on the table. "I'm afraid the news isn't good. The maid who disappeared during the ball was found floating in the Thames early this morning."

Abigail let out a gasp and put her hand to her mouth. A chill crawled up her spine and settled, spiderlike, at the base of her skull.

"There is more. Your father called on Lord Wrexham this morning. The murdered girl was Lady Jane's maid and much regarded by the family. Jane is naturally distraught."

Numbness crept through her, rendering her limbs heavy and awkward. Her lips trembled. Mama had not been with her the previous evening when Robert had announced the disappearance of Jane's maid. Now she had confirmation that the victim was indeed the girl she saw him with in the dark corridor. Was it possible that he had been involved in her disappearance?

Abigail skimmed the article in the *Post*. The paper contained only a perfunctory factual account of the maid's age and disappearance, but the scandal sheets she discovered underneath it had not shown the same restraint. She allowed herself a second scan of the articles, but they did not improve with repetition.

> *What ought to have been a joyous betrothal ball at Wrexham House turned deadly when young Lady J's maid disappeared and was discovered floating in the Thames this morning. Lord H is reported to have been seen in a dark corridor arguing with the maid prior to her disappearance.*

So she hadn't been the only one to witness Robert with the maid. The sheet continued, but Abigail didn't have the fortitude to read it again. Sensing her disquiet, Baxter nudged her hand and she rubbed his head absently. It had been bad enough to discover that Robert had a mistress, but she could not forever tie herself to someone who might be a murderer.

"Mama, the Robert I knew would never have hurt someone. But I…I also saw him in the corridor with the maid."

She stiffened. "Why didn't you tell me?"

"Because I didn't know what to think. Robert has been away for so long. I don't want to believe him capable of hurting someone, but how can I be sure? What am I to do?"

Mama squeezed her hand. "As I said, your father has already spoken with Lord Wrexham, who is convinced of Robert's innocence and has hired a Bow Street runner to investigate the murder and find the killer. Though Robert is not in any real danger of being found guilty of the crime, Wrexham wants his name cleared so there is no doubt in anyone's mind."

"But how am I to ignore the questions in my own mind?" Lord Wrexham might be convinced of his son's innocence, but Abigail was not. She had to tell Mama that she couldn't marry Robert. "Mama, I…I am not in love with Robert."

"Of course you aren't, darling. Love does not bloom quickly. It takes time and careful cultivation. For now, you shall have to be patient and let the runner do as he was hired to do, and in the meantime, you can reacquaint yourself with Robert. Lord Wrexham has asked for our support through this difficult time. His family will be put through much scrutiny and no doubt subjected to malicious gossip, but your father and I are confident they will emerge unscathed from this incident."

Abigail met Mama's eyes, unsure how to proceed.

"We may decide to delay the wedding if Robert's name isn't cleared immediately, but I am certain the runner will do his job and find the murderer quickly."

Abigail nodded. Mama was convinced of Robert's innocence, so she should be, too. But she was the one who was supposed to spend her life with him, and she wasn't convinced. It was all too much.

If she had so many doubts now, there was no hope that their marriage could be successful.

Abigail excused herself and went in search of her father, who she found in the study.

He glanced up as she entered. "You have heard the news, then."

"Yes, Papa." She sat in the chair across from him, grateful

for the warmth of the fire in the hearth. "I want to cry off."

The smile dropped from his face. "Absolutely not. I understand that you are upset, but we must stand by Robert and his family. If you cry off, everyone will believe that you think he is guilty."

"Then they would be right. I do think he is guilty. I saw him in the corridor with his mistress before the ball."

"So that means he must be a murderer?"

She shook her head. "I don't know. But he is not the person I thought he was and I no longer wish to be his wife."

Papa sighed. "I must insist that you remain betrothed to Robert."

Abigail focused her gaze on the dancing flames in the hearth. Perhaps she owed Robert that much. She would never marry him, but she could continue to support him until the murder was solved. It might help quell the scandal that was sure to envelop them both. "Very well, Papa. I will maintain our engagement until the investigation ends."

"That is all I'm asking of you for now. I'm sure you'll feel differently once this mess is sorted out."

Abigail was not going to change her mind about Robert, but there was no point in arguing with Papa. He would think her desire to make a love match was nonsense. Her only course of action was to investigate herself so she could secure her freedom as soon as possible. There was only one person she could think of who would help her and could be trusted not to reveal Abigail's doubts, so she called for Judith to accompany her on the short walk to Georgiana's house.

The butler sent Judith to the kitchen and showed Abigail into the morning room, where Georgiana and Henrietta were engaged in what appeared to be a lively debate.

Abigail stood just inside the door. "My apologies. Am I interrupting?"

Georgiana stood to greet her. "Of course not." She motioned for Abigail to take a seat. "Perhaps you can settle our argument. Henrietta thinks I must marry this season or risk being labeled a spinster. Do you agree?" She raised her brows.

Abigail sat on a settee upholstered in gold silk and looked from Georgiana to Henrietta and back again. "Having been in a similar situation myself barely a fortnight ago, I'm afraid this isn't my area of expertise."

"But surely you have an opinion," Henrietta said.

Abigail smiled at Georgiana. "Seeing as how we are the same age, I can scarcely consider you a spinster."

"Ha!" Georgiana said to Henrietta.

"Be that as it may," Henrietta said, "it is time for you to apply yourself to finding a husband. Now that the war seems to be drawing to a close, you will have the choice of all the available men in London and those returning from the continent. Your options will not change much if you wait, yet you will continue to grow older."

Georgiana laughed. "Such a beacon of hope and light you are, Hen."

Henrietta did not smile. "I am trying to be sensible."

"Yet I know you don't want me to make a hasty decision. I am certain I shall recognize the right man when he comes along. In the meantime, I shall continue to search."

At that moment, Abigail realized that she had been hasty in agreeing to marry Robert without insisting on a period of courtship. They had grown up together, but that didn't change the fact that they had not spent significant time together for several years. He had changed dramatically from the boy she had known.

Georgiana glanced at the newspaper on the table. "Abigail, have you heard about the poor girl pulled from the river this morning?"

She clasped her hands together to stem the trembling. "I'm afraid I have. Remember when I told you about overhearing a maid being propositioned at the ball last night?"

Georgiana nodded. "Of course. That's not the sort of thing I would forget."

"She was the girl who was pulled from the river." She registered the look of shock on both Georgiana's and Henrietta's faces.

Georgiana studied Abigail, her eyes trailing down to observe her tightly clenched, trembling hands. "There was nothing in the paper linking her to Lord Wrexham's household." She turned and rang the bell.

The rare, late afternoon sunlight streaming brightly through the west facing windows of the room was, for once, unable to lift Abigail's dire mood.

A maid arrived and quickly retreated to carry out Georgiana's request for tea.

Georgiana sat next to Abigail and took her hand. "There is more, is there not?"

Abigail nodded. "It was Robert I overheard with the maid just before the dancing started." Her voice broke.

Her friend moved closer and put her arm around Abigail. "What are you going to do?"

"I don't know. My father made me promise to stand by him until the murder is solved. It is the honorable thing to do."

Henrietta gasped and both Abigail and Georgiana turned toward her. Her face was pale, her eyes wide, and her hands trembled in her lap. "Abigail. You mustn't marry him. You cannot risk it."

"Henrietta, he is not Albert. We mustn't jump to conclusions." Georgiana stood and paced across the room. "Abigail, how do you know the dead girl is the maid from Robert's house?"

She held her hands firmly in her lap, determined to maintain control of herself. "Have you not read the scandal sheets? The girl was his sister's maid. And I'm not the only one who witnessed them together in the corridor."

Georgiana ceased her pacing only when the tea arrived. She poured a cup, added a generous quantity of sugar, and pressed it into Abigail's hands. "Has Robert admitted to you that he was carrying on with the maid?" she asked.

Abigail nearly choked on the sip of tea she had just taken and narrowly avoided splattering it all over Georgiana. "Of course not. I didn't tell him that I had seen him with her in the corridor."

"Are you certain it was him?" Georgiana met her eyes.

Abigail nodded. "I'm certain. He disappeared for a long period of time after our first dance last night, and when he returned, he apologized for his absence and said that Lady Jane's maid was missing."

Georgiana placed her hands on her hips. "Has he come to you today to explain?"

"No." What did that say about the possibility of a future between them? Shouldn't she have been the first person he sought? Shouldn't *he* be the one to ask her for her support, and not his father?

"We will have to conduct our own investigation," Henrietta said. "There is no other way to be certain. We cannot trust the authorities."

Abigail carefully set her cup on the table. "I confess I came here today to ask you to help me do just that. But how are we to proceed?"

"We will have to get Edmund involved," said Georgiana.

Abigail leapt from her seat. "No. Robert would never forgive me for spreading word of the incident among society."

Georgiana took her hand. "Dearest, there is no way to prevent the flood of gossip that will disseminate among the *ton*, especially in light of the information already circulated by the scandal sheets. Edmund is to be trusted, and he has entree to places and information we cannot access. We need his assistance."

She considered the truth in Georgiana's words. Her brother had been charming at the ball, and he seemed trustworthy, though certainly she had reason to question her own judgment. "Very well, but we must be discrete."

Georgiana squeezed her hand. "Of course. There is no one more trustworthy than Edmund."

Abigail agreed. This was the best way to proceed, and likely her only option to solve the murder and end her betrothal to Robert quickly. She had only to look to Henrietta to know that it was better not to marry at all than to be trapped in an unhappy marriage.

Chapter Three

Edmund sat at a table facing the window, furiously scribbling sums on a sheet of foolscap, when a knock sounded and the door creaked open. "Put the tea on my desk," he said without raising his head.

"I'm afraid we haven't brought you tea," Georgiana said.

He turned and stood when he caught sight of Henrietta. For the thousandth time, regret washed over him. He wished he had known of her husband's violent tendencies. "Hen, to what do I owe the pleasure of your company?"

Georgiana fiddled with the ledger on his desk. "She stopped by to harangue me about securing a husband this season, but we find that there are other, more pressing issues to be dealt with."

Before he could respond, Lady Abigail appeared behind Henrietta, her green eyes vivid in contrast to her pale skin. He thought back to some of her previous visits with his family, and how she somehow always managed to make everyone feel at ease, and wished he could do the same for her today. "Lady Abigail. Welcome."

"Thank you, my lord. My apologies for interrupting your work."

"It is no bother." He added the chair he had been using to the two in front of his desk and motioned to the ladies to be seated. He sat behind his desk, one brow raised in question.

Georgiana, the more outgoing of his two eldest sisters, spoke. "A maid employed by Lord Wrexham disappeared from the ball last night. She was found floating in the Thames this morning."

He leaned back in his chair. "That is unfortunate, but I fail to see how it is a pressing issue for us."

Georgiana straightened in her chair. "Abigail witnessed Lord Hinsdale engaged in...well...propositioning the maid in question during the ball last night, as did someone else, because it was all over the scandal sheets this morning."

He raised one brow. "And?"

"Edmund, do stop being so obtuse. He was propositioning the maid, and she refused him. Now she is dead." She narrowed her eyes at him.

Henrietta leaned forward. "Abigail is betrothed to Lord Hinsdale. We must investigate and determine if it is safe for her to marry him."

Ah. He did rather like Lady Abigail. She sat silently, unmoving, watching the interplay between his sisters and him, her pale face unsmiling. It would not do to have her married to a murderer. "Then by all means, conduct your investigation. I assume I don't need to remind you to be discreet."

"Edmund!" Georgiana leapt from her chair and paced toward the window. She'd never excelled at remaining still. "You must help us."

It was bad of him, but he did enjoy taunting Georgiana. "What information do we have?"

Lady Abigail spoke first. "She was Lady Jane's maid, and it appears that she was also Lord Hinsdale's mistress. My father spoke with Lord Wrexham this morning, and he has hired a Bow Street runner to find the murderer and clear his son's name."

Edmund considered the circumstances. That was a hell of a way to start a marriage. He certainly didn't wish for one of his sisters to endure such a situation, but it wasn't his place to advise Lady Abigail. "Then why should we become involved? We will simply have to wait for the runner to finish his investigation."

Abigail met his gaze, her eyes wide. "My lord, no matter what the runner determines, I must know whether he is guilty." She glanced down. "I cannot stand by a man who may have committed murder."

A surge of protectiveness pulsed through him. Of course he had to help her. "I will investigate. Is there any other information available?"

Georgiana handed him the *Post* and he quickly skimmed the article while the ladies remained uncharacteristically silent. "There were no possessions found with the body. Do we know if she left the house voluntarily, or if she planned to return?"

Lady Abigail shook her head. "I hadn't even considered the possibility that she might have been forced to leave. If Lord Wrexham found out she had been carrying on with his son, he might have dismissed her." Her eyes narrowed. "All we know for sure is that she left the house sometime after the ball started last night."

"Do you know anyone who went to school with Hinsdale?" Georgiana asked him.

He plunked his elbow onto the desk and leaned his chin on his palm, attempting to calculate how long the investigation would take. His sisters would need to be monitored. Especially Georgiana. "Not offhand."

"I don't suppose there's any point in asking you to allow me to handle the investigation?" He made eye contact with Georgiana as he spoke.

She shook her head. "None whatsoever."

"Duly noted." He stood and strolled to the window, ruminating over the best way to complete the investigation quickly. "If we operate on the assumption that Hinsdale is innocent, then we must search for other suspects. I believe Woolford has a cousin or some such in service at Wrexham House. Perhaps he can discover who the maid's acquaintances were within the household. In the meantime, I will do some sleuthing at my club to determine whether Hinsdale should be considered a suspect. We will have to wait for more information to come out in the papers."

"And the scandal sheets," Georgiana added.

Lady Abigail nodded. "I will speak with Lady Jane as well. Hopefully she will have more information about the girl's departure."

Edmund was pleased to see some color on Lady Abigail's face. "Very well. Would you please ask Woolford to join me?"

"Certainly," said Georgiana.

The ladies all stood and headed toward the door.

"Will you stay for dinner, Hen?" he asked over his shoulder.

She shot him a rare, genuine smile. "If you'd like. I haven't any engagements this evening."

"Mother will be pleased." He turned toward them. "Lady Abigail, you are welcome as well."

"I thank you, my lord, but I believe I am needed at home."

"Yes, of course." He had thought she might enjoy a respite from her situation, but of course she would want to be at home with her own family. He tilted his head toward his sisters. "I assume you will expect a full report of my findings."

Georgiana smiled. "You plan to work quickly, then."

"The sooner I start, the sooner I finish."

The ladies took their leave and a knock sounded moments later.

Edmund sat behind his desk. "Enter."

Woolford pushed through the doorway and bowed. "You requested my presence, my lord?"

"Please sit," he said, gesturing to a chair. When Woolford had made himself comfortable, he spoke. "Do you have any knowledge of Viscount Hinsdale?"

Woolford sat ramrod straight on the edge of the chair. Comfortable was a relative term. "I haven't had the pleasure of meeting him, my lord."

Edmund leaned back and put his feet up on the desk, hoping Woolford would read his signal to be easy. "From what I understand, he likely wouldn't be much of a pleasure to meet."

One side of Woolford's mouth curved ever so slightly.

That was likely about as relaxed as he could manage.

"Doesn't your cousin work for Lord Wrexham?"

"Yes, my lord. He is a footman."

"What sort of man is your cousin? Would he be willing to speak with me about Lord Hinsdale, or do you think he would be more at ease speaking with you?" The telltale patter of rain hit the window behind him, putting an end to the sunshine. Perhaps it would be a good day to seek the sanctuary of White's.

"May I be free with you, my lord?"

Edmund pulled his feet from the desk and sat up. "Always."

Woolford's lips clamped together tightly, as if he would rather not speak. "Do you think he killed the maid?"

"So it is common knowledge already." Edmund rubbed his temples. The ladies had said something about scandal sheets, so he shouldn't be surprised that the news had circulated quickly. That would make his work more difficult, as it would be even more necessary to be discreet. And it would require more time. Time he didn't wish to spare. However, he would not quit until Lady Abigail had the answers she needed.

Woolford nodded. "I'm afraid so, my lord. Front page of the scandal papers this afternoon."

Edmund spun the ledger on his desk as he thought out loud. "I am interested in your cousin's opinion about Lord Hinsdale's character. Hinsdale is betrothed to Lady Georgiana's friend, and she is naturally concerned for her friend's welfare. So it is up to us to determine whether, in light of the circumstances, it is still a wise match."

"I understand, my lord, and think it best that I speak with my cousin without mentioning your involvement. Might even be able to speak with some of the other servants."

"A first-rate idea. I will go to my club to see what I can discover there. Please report back to me when you are able to secure any relevant information. I am most interested in who was friendly to the girl. Or if there was anyone who was not. Anyone who might have had a reason to want her gone from the household."

Woolford nodded and stood. "If I may say, my lord, it's quite decent of you to make sure Lady Georgiana's friend will be safe. I am honored to be included." He bowed and turned to leave.

"Woodford," Edmund called after him, "you are an integral part of this investigation, and don't you forget it. Nothing in this house would work without you." Woodford's shoulders straightened and he strode firmly through the doorway, closing the door softly behind him, his purpose renewed.

. . .

Edmund took another swallow of brandy and peered over the top of his newspaper. White's was normally a place of calm, quiet, comfort, and tranquility. Dominated by dark wood paneling, thick carpets, lush upholstery, and a roaring fire, it was the place he sought when he needed peace and serenity. Not so today. Today it was abuzz over the murder of Lord Wrexham's maid. He glanced back at the article in the afternoon paper. Ligature marks on the victim's neck assured it was a murder and not an accident, but the question was, why did she flee Lord Wrexham's house? And, who would want to harm her? Edmund thought it wise to feign disinterest and see what information he could glean from the conversations around him.

No sooner had he raised the paper than Lord Oakley plunked down in the chair opposite him.

"Oakley." He nodded and went back to his paper.

"Longcroft." Oakley returned his nod. "I understand you attended the Wrexham ball last night. Did you notice anything unusual?"

Edmund set the paper on the table and took another gulp of brandy. He would need fortification to deal with Oakley. "I witnessed a great many unusual things. Shadowed figures skulking about the garden, whispered conversations in dark corners of the ballroom, even a spat between a well-known duke and his mistress."

Oakley's less than ample lips thinned into a barely perceptible line. "I meant, anything unusual with regard to the murder."

"Ah." Edmund nodded again. "I'm certain you've read the papers, so you'll know the murder didn't occur at the ball."

Oakley leaned closer. "So you didn't see anything unusual?"

The man was nothing if not persistent. "I'm afraid not."

Oakley scanned the area around them before speaking again. "Surely something out of the ordinary must have happened to cause the girl to flee."

"That is certainly a possibility, but lady's maids don't frequent the ballroom, so it's nothing the guests would have been privy to." Edmund wiped a bead of condensation from his glass with the pad of his index finger. "You'd likely have better luck questioning the servants than the guests. Regardless of what caused her to flee, there must be someone in that house who knows."

"Good point." Oakley smoothed his hair and glanced around the room, likely searching for his next target to interrogate.

Edmund rapped his hand against the table. "I know everyone is speculating as to what happened, but I think it's entirely possible that the girl simply decided to pursue other interests and was the unlucky target of footpads."

A gleam shone in Oakley's eyes and he changed his tactics. "Would you care to wager on whether a member of the Wrexham family is involved?"

Oakley wasn't known for being particularly clever, so Edmund took a chance. "You know something, don't you?" He met Oakley's eyes and held them until Oakley squirmed in his seat and pulled at his cravat. "Come now. Do share."

Oakley focused his gaze at the fireplace. "If I share my information with you, you won't take the wager."

He raised his brows. "Have you ever known me to wager?"

He shifted his eyes back to Edmund. "Come to think of it, no. Why is that?"

Edmund leaned forward and rested his elbows on the table. "I have six younger sisters. Six. That means six dowries. I haven't a farthing to spare."

Oakley smirked. "We all know you're flush, Longcroft."

"Because I don't wager." He leaned back in his chair. "I'm certain you'll be able to find someone here who will."

"Oh, I don't think that will be a problem," he said, grinning widely. "The first wager was recorded in the betting book over an hour ago. Everyone knows Lord Wrexham has hired a Bow Street runner to solve the murder and clear his son's name, and the coroner has been at the house all day, questioning the servants."

Edmund sank into his chair, debating whether this would make it easier or more difficult for him to conduct his investigation. Any hope of concluding the matter quickly was long gone.

"Now that you know nothing will entice me to make a wager, would you care to share your information?"

Oakley sighed. "I suppose it can't hurt. I was at Cambridge with Hinsdale. Lived across the corridor from him."

"And?" Edmund prompted when he stopped talking.

"Let's just say that he was reprimanded more than once for being caught with a female in his chamber."

Edmund suspected that allegation applied to many members of the *ton*. He raised a brow. "Is that all?"

Oakley leaned back in his chair. "Well, no, though I should think it would be enough to cast suspicion on him. He was also known for having a quick temper, especially with the servants."

"I see. Thank you for your insight." Sighing to himself, he rose from his chair and made his way to the betting book.

A quick glance at the current page revealed two bets regarding Hinsdale, one of which supported his innocence, and the other, his guilt. Interestingly, both wagers had originated with Lord Diller, who was blatantly hedging his bets. The odds were currently two-to-one that Hinsdale was innocent.

One thing was certain. Whether Hinsdale was guilty or not, this would be the scandal of the season.

Chapter Four

Abigail sighed as she skimmed the scandal sheets, which held no new information but merely speculated as to the progress of the investigation and the likelihood of Robert's guilt. She would not have had to rely solely on them for information if he would deign to visit her. She had not seen him in nearly two days, since the night of the ball, and although she didn't want to believe he was guilty, the longer he stayed away, the more she contemplated why he was avoiding her. Of course he should feel guilty for embroiling her in his indiscretions, but the situation could do nothing but fester as long as he stayed away. Not only did he not turn to her for comfort or reassurance, but he didn't seem to care enough about her to even try to explain his actions or gauge her reaction to the situation he had thrust them both into.

His absence did, however, cement her decision not to marry him.

Papa had canceled their plans to attend the theater

the previous evening, hoping the furor over the murder would die down, but of course it had only grown. Mama had insisted that they be at home for callers today. Though Abigail agreed that they could not hide forever, a few more days of seclusion would have been her preference.

The creak of the front door heralded the arrival of their first visitor. Not wanting to draw unnecessary attention, Abigail shoved the scandal sheets in the drawer of a side table. Relief flowed through her at the sound of Georgiana's voice, though she had not arrived alone. Deep, masculine tones that did not belong to Williams, the butler, carried down the corridor. Her stomach fluttered. Lord Longcroft had accompanied Georgiana. The deep tone of his voice soothed her nerves. Abigail stood and brushed imaginary wrinkles from her gown. Baxter wagged his tail when Mama swept into the parlor.

"Good heavens, you are as pale as Lord Elgin's statues. Hurry, pinch your cheeks before our guests enter."

Mama dropped onto the settee and she followed suit. Normally she would have picked up a book or her embroidery so as not to appear idle, but Georgiana would be fooled by neither.

Williams strode to the threshold to announce their guests. Georgiana had brought her brother with her. Though the show of support was appreciated, his presence did nothing to calm her nerves.

Dispensing with formality, Georgiana hugged Abigail and dropped into the chair beside her, while the marquess moved to greet them properly.

"Lady Jaffrey, how delightful to see you again." He bowed over Mama's hand.

"Lord Longcroft, you are quite welcome." Mama waved

a hand at the chair across from her. "Please, make yourself comfortable."

"Lady Abigail." He clasped her hand, his warm grip penetrating through her glove, causing her stomach to flutter. He took the seat Mama had indicated and glanced at Georgiana with raised brows.

Before even Mama could produce an appropriate topic to discuss, her closest friend, Lady Nightinger, was announced, along with Lord Oakley. Though Abigail had danced with Oakley a handful of times, he had never had any real interest in her, which was just fine since he was a known gossip and an active gambler. It was widely suspected that someday soon he would involve himself in a scrape from which his father would not be able to extract him. Since Abigail had no memory of him ever calling upon them at home before, he was clearly here to glean as much information as possible from them about Robert.

"Lady Abigail, how are you faring?" Lord Oakley asked.

"I am quite well, thank you," she answered, unsure what else her mother would deem permissible.

"Excellent. Were you able to locate a copy of the second edition of *Children's and Household Tales*?"

Here she had been condemning him, when she had completely forgotten about their shared love of fairy tales. Perhaps he wasn't all bad, just overly curious. "Not yet, but Mr. Cross has assured me he will have one for me soon. I thank you for the suggestion, my lord. I'm quite eager to compare the stories with those of Perrault."

"That should be an interesting proposition. You are lucky to have had a German governess. Perhaps you should endeavor to create an English translation for those who are not so lucky."

Abigail suppressed a giggle at the thought. "You are too kind, my lord. I doubt my skills are up to the task, but it would be delightful for the book to be made available in English."

"Indeed." He glanced toward Mama. "If you'll excuse me, I must pay my respects to Lady Jaffrey."

Noting the increasing number of people continuing to arrive, Baxter sidled up to her and sat atop her feet. Lord Longcroft glanced her way at the movement and lifted his brows, then turned back to answer Lord Oakley's question.

Abigail smiled and fixed her gaze on Baxter while attempting to overhear their conversation.

"Surely you can't think the man completely innocent. If nothing else, he is guilty of having a dalliance with the wrong woman," said Lord Oakley.

"Oakley, might I remind you that you are in the company of ladies," Lord Longcroft said in low tones not meant for her ears.

"Yes, of course." He smiled inanely at Abigail, but continued to push for information.

"Does he never give up?" Georgiana whispered in her ear.

"I suspect not." His love of fairy tales aside, it seemed her first assessment of Oakley had been correct after all. Abigail wished there were more ladies present. Georgiana and Lady Nightinger were the only females in the room, save Abigail and her mother. Likely they wanted to stay far away from the scandal that plagued her.

Oakley smacked his hands together, startling Baxter, who shot from Abigail's feet into the middle of the crowd. He spun around, eyes wide.

"Baxter," Abigail called, but the crowd had shifted around him and he couldn't see her. He whined and spun about again. She stood, but couldn't make her way through the crush to reach him. Georgiana's brother pushed through the crowd toward her dog and knelt down, making an odd cooing sound. Baxter went to him, placed his front feet on his legs, and licked his face.

Abigail slapped her hand over her mouth, waiting to see how he would respond.

"You silly beast. You're a hound. How could you have lost track of your mistress?"

Baxter licked him again, and Lord Longcroft rubbed his ears, grasped his collar, and led him over to her. "Lady Abigail, he seems to have lost track of you in the crush."

"So it would seem. Thank you, my lord." Though Baxter's disability rarely affected him, he sometimes panicked when he was unable to see her. Lord Longcroft's kindness spread warmth through her. Though he had always been thoughtful on the few occasions she had the opportunity to speak with him, she sensed there was much more to him than Georgiana had conveyed to her. There was something so comforting about his presence and the ease with which he solved problems without a fuss. If only Robert was more like him. Alas, he was not and never would be, and Long Longecroft had six sisters to marry off before he would even consider a match of his own.

Abigail sat and Baxter jumped onto the settee, eliciting a glare from Mama, who did not allow Baxter on the furniture because she disliked having dog hair on her gowns. Abigail wondered briefly if she could chase Oakley away with a threat of dog hair spoiling his coat, but it would likely take more than that to oust him.

As if he could sense her thoughts, Lord Oakley turned his attention to her. "Lady Abigail, you must be devastated."

Abigail pretended not to understand his question. "I am quite well, thank you, my lord."

His eyes narrowed, most likely because he was attempting to devise a polite way to question her. "Excellent. I was afraid you had taken ill when I didn't see you at the theater last night."

Georgiana's eyes narrowed at his poorly veiled inquiry, but Abigail remained determined to show no weakness. "I thank you for your concern, my lord, but all is well. I'm afraid my father is not a great fan of the opera, and he rarely enjoys spending two nights in a row away from home. I'm sure you understand."

He stiffened. "Of course, my lady."

Abigail went on the offensive, secure in her knowledge of the one thing that would deter him from questioning her further. "My lord, I hope you don't think me too bold, but I have long expected to hear news of you making a favorable match. After all, you have been dallying on the marriage mart for quite some time. Do tell me, are you close to making an offer? Your name has lately been linked to Lord Gromley's daughter." Lord Gromley's daughter who, though possessed of a rather large fortune, was unfortunately nearly as wide as she was tall.

Oakley sucked in a breath as if to speak, then coughed vehemently. Longcroft winked at Abigail before pounding him on the back for good measure.

She grinned back at him. He was a good man to have on her side.

Chapter Five

Abigail had finally fallen asleep mere moments before she received word that Robert awaited her presence in the parlor. Though she had wondered why he hadn't called on her sooner, she was tired after spending the afternoon deflecting Oakley's inappropriate attempts to glean information from her, and she had hoped to rest for a few hours before it was time to dress for the Abbott ball. After splashing some water on her face and checking her hair, she hurried down the staircase and rushed into the parlor with Baxter at her heels. Both Robert and Papa stood.

"Hello, darling." Papa kissed her cheek. "I shall leave you two to your discussion."

Abigail's eyes widened as her father strode from the room. She hadn't expected to be left alone with Robert, though she supposed it was permissible since they were betrothed. Still, Papa left the door open, causing her to wonder how confident he was about Robert's innocence. She sat on the settee and folded her hands across her lap, waiting for Robert to explain his presence after staying away for so long. Baxter settled next to her feet.

He sat next to her on the settee and took her hand. "I wish to apologize for my absence. It was unforgivably rude of me not to call on you sooner."

She definitely agreed that it was rude, though there was no purpose in voicing that to him. Instead, she smiled. "I wouldn't say that your behavior was unforgivable."

"Thank you." He squeezed her hands, but rather than finding it soothing, it unnerved her. "It's just that both the magistrate and the coroner questioned me yesterday about Lady Jane's maid." He looked down for a moment. "It wasn't a pleasant experience, but my father thinks it best to cooperate fully with the authorities, and he has hired a Bow Street runner to investigate on our behalf."

She squeezed his hand and waited for him to continue. In her heart she wanted him to be innocent, and she could support him despite the fact that she no longer wished to marry him.

"I wanted you to hear this from me before the news was made public, but I'm certain you've already seen the gossip sheets."

She held his gaze, anticipating what he was about to say, but not willing to make it any easier for him. Since they were still betrothed, he owed her the courtesy of telling her himself.

"I am sorry that you have to even know about this, but the maid was my mistress."

Abigail swallowed against the knot in her throat. Did he think her a simpleton? How could he think she didn't already know? She cast her eyes downward, away from him. She briefly considered telling him that she had seen him in the corridor with the maid at their betrothal ball. But the niggling possibility that he could be guilty kept her from speaking out.

Robert placed a finger under her chin and turned her to meet his eyes. "I did not kill her. I would never have deliberately hurt her." He glanced out the open door to the corridor and whispered, "I loved her."

Nausea billowed in her stomach. She had expected his admission that the maid was his mistress, but she had not expected him to confess to feelings that undermined their entire relationship. "Robert, I don't understand. Why did you ask me to marry you if you were in love with another woman?" Clearly, he had a very different idea of what marriage should be if he thought love for each other didn't have a place in it.

With an agitated expression crossing his face, Robert stood and paced to the window. Both she and Baxter followed his movements with their eyes. "Abigail, you know our parents have expected us to marry since we were children." He ran his fingers through his hair. "I don't quite know how to explain this to you. I loved Sarah, but of course I would never have married her." He turned to her and shrugged. "A future earl does not marry a maid. It just isn't done." He moved back to the settee, but thankfully did not attempt to hold her hand. "My feelings for her had nothing to do with our marriage and would not have affected it. I never intended for her to be anything more than my mistress."

Could he have become enraged and killed the maid when she told him she was leaving? The Robert she had grown up with would never have hurt someone, but she barely recognized this man.

She focused on breathing in and out for a moment. Though Abigail was horrified by the murder, there was nothing she could do to change what had happened. She had already made the decision not to marry Robert, and she would not change her mind. But she was curious. "Do you intend to seek out another mistress, then?"

Robert strode back to her and pulled a missive from his pocket. "Abigail, my relationship with Sarah was not simply a matter of…a matter of convenience. I did love her." He ran his fingers through his hair. "Here, read this." He thrust a note into her hands.

She took a deep breath and unfolded the paper, carefully smoothing it against her lap. Abigail's heart clenched. Some of the words were smudged where the maid's tears had dropped onto the page.

> *Dearest,*
>
> *I am leaving Wrexham House tonight. You claim to love me, and yet you marry another. I cannot stand by and watch you make a life with her and expect me to live in the shadows, an afterthought, only seeing you when you are able to steal away from your family for brief periods. This is not how I want to live my life. I want a family and children of my own. Do not try to find me. I do not wish to see you again.*

Numbness crept through her, its tentacles wrapping around her and chilling her to the bone. She stood and strode to the fireplace. "Did you show this to the authorities?"

"Yes, the magistrate read it and agreed it was proof that she left the house voluntarily."

She placed her hands on her hips. "Did he suspect you of following her?"

"Though my father would not allow Jane to be questioned by the magistrate, he did ask her himself when she last saw Sarah. It was at the beginning of the ball, and there were several witnesses to my whereabouts at that time." Robert stood and paced toward the window. "The servants are being questioned, and several of them have corroborated that I was in the ballroom at the time Sarah left the house."

Abigail was too numb to form a response. Random thoughts swirled inside her head, making it difficult to speak. The poor girl had only wanted the same things she herself wanted.

"I asked your father if he would be willing to speak with the runner. We both agree that you should be exempt from the investigations, but your father intends to cooperate fully. He can attest to the fact that I was present in the ballroom until long after Sarah left the house."

"But you were missing for quite a long time after that." The thought slipped from her mouth, unbidden.

Robert's eyes narrowed. "That was when one of the footmen delivered Sarah's note. I attempted to locate her but was told that she had already left. I needed time to compose myself before returning to the ball."

"Yes, of course you did." Baxter leaned against her leg and she stroked his head. But Robert was the only one who knew for sure whether he had left the house to look for

Sarah. Even if one of the servants had seen him leave, it was unlikely he or she would speak out against him for fear of being dismissed.

Robert met her eyes, then knelt before her and took both of her hands. "Abigail, I swear to you that I had nothing to do with her death. I need you to believe that."

She wanted to believe him, thought back to all of their adventures as children. But there were still far too many unanswered questions. For a moment, she considered telling him she wanted to cry off, but she had promised Papa she would not, and their longstanding friendship compelled her to continue to support him for the time being. "I don't believe you to be a killer, Robert."

He released a pent up breath.

"Do they have any other suspects?" she asked.

"Not yet. I'm hoping once the runner speaks with your father and a few other guests from the ball, the authorities will be convinced to direct their efforts toward finding the real killer."

She turned to meet his eyes. "Do you have any idea who it could have been?"

"I suspect she was set upon by footpads and their attempt to rob her went awry." He smiled. "She wasn't one to give in easily and would have fought back for all she was worth. I think she truly believed I would change my mind and marry her." He shook his head. "As if I could marry a maid. As if my father would allow it."

Abigail felt as if she had been doused with a bucket of cold water. Robert claimed that he had loved poor Sarah, and yet he could laugh about how silly she had been to think he would marry her. He didn't seem to understand what love meant.

"Abigail, will you stand by me?" He lifted her chin and looked into her eyes. "I need your support now more than ever."

She nodded. "I will continue to support your innocence."

Robert released his pent up breath and laid his head in her lap. Baxter popped up immediately and shoved his head next to Robert's and pushed at her hand, hoping to receive his share of her attention. She smiled in spite of herself, but tensed when Robert lifted his head.

"You silly beast," he said, rubbing Baxter's ear, "I suppose I shall need to resign myself to your constant interference."

Relief flooded her and washed away some of the tension in her neck. Something of the Robert from her childhood was still there, but it wasn't enough to convince her that they could make a happy life together.

After seeing Robert out, Abigail headed to her father's study. She knocked and pushed the door open to peek inside.

"Come in, my dear. How are you holding up?"

She walked to his desk slowly, relaxing a bit with each step. The fire crackled merrily and the cozy comfort of the room soothed her battered spirit.

"I am fine. I just wish I could be certain of Robert's innocence." She sat in one of the armchairs that faced his desk and smoothed her skirts. "Do you think him capable of murder?"

"Anyone is capable of murder when forced into certain situations, but I do not believe that he would have hurt the maid."

That wasn't exactly a resounding show of support. "Robert said you are to speak with the runner Lord Wrexham hired to investigate the murder."

Papa's eyes narrowed, but he nodded. "I have agreed to meet with him in the morning, though I don't see what I could possibly add to the investigation."

She glanced down at her hands. "Papa, I should like to speak to the runner."

"Absolutely not." His tone left no room for argument. "There is no place for a lady in a murder inquest." He relaxed against his chair. "Normally I would be exempt from speaking with him as well, but we are hoping to put this matter behind us as quickly as possible so I have agreed to be interviewed."

She kept her head down. "Yes, Papa."

He drew in a deep breath. "Do you know something that might be of use to the runner in his investigation?"

A small thrill of victory shot through her. "Just after we arrived at the ball, I witnessed Robert in the corridor with the maid. He had her trapped against the wall and she was crying and begging him to release her so she could attend to his sister."

He drew his brows together. "That doesn't necessarily mean anything. It is already common knowledge that they had a relationship, and that she was distraught over the betrothal. Another witness to their…interlude in the corridor was quoted in the gossip sheets."

Abigail cleared her throat. Unbidden guilt pressed against her despite her previous lack of knowledge about the girl's relationship with Robert. Yet, had she not accepted his offer, the maid would still be alive.

"Papa, when are you to meet with the runner?"

His eyes narrowed.

"In case I think of something else you should share with him," she clarified.

"He is to call on me tomorrow morning."

"Thank you." She made her way around his desk and kissed his cheek.

He wrapped her into a hug. "I'm sorry to have to put you through this, pigeon, but you know that Lord Wrexham is one of my closest friends, and I still believe Robert is a good match for you. This will soon be behind us."

"Yes, Papa." It would serve no purpose to tell her father how painful it had been for her to hear Robert confess his love for another woman and simply assume she still wanted to marry him, and it was even less productive to wish she could rewind the clock and save the maid. Abigail called to Baxter and retreated to her bedchamber.

Looking for an escape from her situation, she ran her fingers across the spines of several books. Not quite in the mood for *Beauty and the Beast,* she searched for another book. She read the title on the spine of several of the books on her shelves and considered what was preventing her from reading one of her favorite stories. Was it because the story was a bit too similar to her own? Could Robert be a prince in disguise? Or was he really a beast at heart? She wasn't willing to risk marrying him to find out.

Her thoughts returned to her conversation with Papa. The runner was coming in the morning, and she intended to be privy to his questioning. If they met in the study it would be no problem as she and George, the eldest of her younger brothers, had long ago discovered a convenient place to eavesdrop in the corridor outside the little used servant's entrance at the back of the chamber. But if they met in the parlor, her task would be more difficult. Perhaps she could hear them through the chimney in the bedchamber above. She would have to enlist George's help.

She pulled Madame D'Aulnoy's book of fairy tales from her bookshelf and settled on the bed. Baxter jumped up and lay next to her, placing his head in her lap. She fondled his ears and tried to absorb herself in the story of Princess Mayblossom, but it was no use. She leaned back and closed her eyes. Mayblossom had at first fallen for the wrong man before she found her true prince. Abigail feared she had done the same, but there would be no other prince coming to rescue her from her fate.

Chapter Six

Later that evening, Abigail was fully dressed and waiting on her parents to leave for the Abbott ball. Though she would rather have had her fingernails pulled out one by one than appear in public, she had accepted Robert's offer of marriage and had agreed to support him through this ordeal, and she would not go back on her word no matter how painful a situation it put her in.

Abigail put much care into choosing her gown for the ball and had selected what was, for her, a simple design. She had chosen white, hoping to show her youth and purity to offset the suspicions about Robert's involvement in the murder.

The gown was saved from being too plain by the addition of lace under-sleeves and sheer over-sleeves, with a pink sash added for a pinch of color. A single strand of pearls adorned her neck. Footsteps on the stairs signaled that her parents were ready to leave

No one spoke as they climbed into the carriage and settled in their seats. They rode the short distance to the ball in thunderous quiet.

She threw out a desperate question as the carriage slowed. "How should I respond if someone asks about the murder? Or Robert's involvement with the maid?"

Papa took her hand. "Say as little as possible, and affirm that you are still betrothed and that Robert is not guilty."

Yes, she could do that. All she had to do was support Robert until the murder was solved and then she would be free.

Mama nodded and fussed with Abigail's shawl, not meeting her eyes.

Clutching her reticle, she followed her parents out of the carriage. They entered the ballroom and relief coursed through her when she spotted Georgiana and Henrietta, a safe haven of people who supported her and would help deflect unwanted attention. She left her parents speaking with their friends and headed to relative safety.

Georgiana reached for her hand. "How are you holding up?" she asked softly.

"As well as can be expected. Luckily I've been through enough seasons to be experienced at hiding my feelings."

Georgiana squeezed her hand and Henrietta smiled in tacit agreement.

Abigail sucked in a deep breath as Robert approached with narrowed eyes and his lips tight with censure. "I had hoped you would arrive earlier," he said in a stage whisper. He clasped her hand. "I need your support."

She glanced around to see if anyone was looking before she spoke. Considering how uncomfortable she was, she should be able to forgive Robert for feeling his nerves. She wiggled her hand to loosen his slightly painful hold. "Papa wanted to avoid the receiving line, but I'm here now."

"Let's take to the dance floor. There's less opportunity there for others to ask questions," Robert said.

She allowed him to lead her away, looking back over her shoulder at Georgiana. If they could just make it through the ball, things would get easier. The gossips would soon come across some other scandal to occupy their time, and hopefully the runner was making progress with his investigations.

The music began and Robert whirled her into a slightly-faster-than-the-music waltz. Abigail deliberately slowed her movements, hoping he would follow suit. It would do none of them any good to have attended the ball if he appeared agitated. Perhaps she could distract him with conversation. She was much more informed about the news than usual since she had been scouring the papers every day for information about the murder.

"What do you think of General Drouot being declared not guilty?"

Robert whipped his head around and his eyes focused on hers. "What? Why would I give a fig about the fate of a French general when my neck might be on the line?"

Suitably chastised, she remained silent for the rest of the dance. She had to remember that whatever discomfort she was feeling was magnified tenfold for him. They received a few curious stares as they moved about the dance floor, but nothing overt. Once the music came to an end, Robert led her back to her mother.

He bowed over her hand. "I am going to the billiard room, but I will return shortly to claim another dance."

Secreting himself in the billiard room might be the best option for Robert, but he didn't seem to care that he was abandoning her to fend for herself. She supposed that was something she would have to become accustomed to once she ended their engagement. Even from the time she made her come out, everyone had known that she was intended for him, so she had never been sought after on the marriage mart. Still, the prospect of a life alone was more appealing to her than marrying Robert.

"He seems a bit agitated," Mama said.

That was a polite understatement, but she could hardly blame him for being out of sorts in such a public forum. Hopefully the runner would find the murderer soon.

Her mother turned away to speak with Lady Holland, and Abigail was left to entertain herself. She scanned the ballroom, searching for someone she could converse with. A few sideways glances were sent her way, but nothing blatant that could be construed as more than curiosity. Abigail kept a serene countenance.

Henrietta was standing nearby and Abigail sidled over to her. Henrietta rarely danced now that she was a widow and was not in the market for a husband. Abigail envied her freedom, though certainly not the circumstances that led to it.

"How are you faring?" Henrietta asked.

"I am soldiering on." She glanced around to make sure no one was within hearing distance before continuing. "Robert is tense this evening, which I suppose is to be expected given the scrutiny he is enduring."

Henrietta briefly met her eyes. "I do hope for your sake that he is innocent. However, he did bring this on himself by carrying on with the maid in the first place."

Abigail understood Henrietta's distrust of men, but it would do her no good to lambast Robert for his indiscretions. What was done was done and could not be undone, so there was no point in dwelling on it.

Henrietta reached over and clasped her hand. "My apologies. Shame on me for adding to the weight you are already shouldering. Everything will work out one way or another. Either he is guilty and you will break off the betrothal, or he is not guilty and will learn from his transgressions."

Abigail drew in a deep breath. The problem was that neither of those options fulfilled the vision of how she had imagined her life, living with her very own fairy tale prince. She wasn't sure what to hope for once she was free of her betrothal to Robert. Was it too much to hope that she might find someone else who could love her?

She spotted Lord Longcroft dancing with Lady Needler and suppressed a grin. She hoped he would avoid being pummeled by her alarmingly vast bosom.

Henrietta followed her line of sight. "She really ought to invest in sturdier stays, don't you think?"

Abigail bit her lip and deliberately avoided meeting Henrietta's eye. The purpose of being here was to not make a spectacle of herself. Still, she shook with silent laughter that would not be repressed.

"I'm glad one of us is having a good time tonight."

Goose pimples scattered across her neck when Robert spoke, as effective in killing her laughter as a slap to the face.

"Shall we?" He held out his hand, presumably asking her for the next dance.

"Yes, of course." She glanced over her shoulder at

Henrietta, whose expression belied her unspoken concern.

Robert clasped her hand so firmly her fingers began to tingle as if being jabbed by needles, and she longed for the times when he had gently stroked her wrist or palm. She wiggled her fingers until his grip relaxed slightly. He remained silent as they maneuvered through the steps of the quadrille, his movements as stiff as his unsmiling face.

She could no longer hold her tongue. "Robert, do take care. I understand that you are under stress and feel unfairly accused, but you are drawing attention to yourself with your taciturn countenance. I thought the point of making an appearance tonight was to show that everything is normal."

His face went pale for a moment before it was suffused by crimson in a way that had heretofore been associated with the onset of scarlet fever. Obviously, she had said the wrong thing, though she was at a loss to know what would have been right. Wasn't it her place to advise him on how others might perceive his behavior?

He met her concerned gaze with narrowed eyes. "If I wish to hear your opinions, I will ask for them. Since I do not, you may remain silent."

So she did, wondering anew how much longer she would have to wait before she could cry off. Again, she scanned the ballroom and found no one paying undue attention to them, though there were always whispered conversations occurring in the shadows at a ball.

A few minutes later, Robert leaned close and murmured "My apologies for speaking that way to you. It was wrong of me to take out my frustrations on you." He looked into her eyes. "Will you forgive me?"

"Of course. There is nothing to forgive." That wasn't

precisely true, but considering how tense she was, she could only imagine what it was like for Robert. Better he snap at her than someone else who might misinterpret his actions.

He returned her to her mother again, and left after a cursory goodbye. Abigail exhaled slowly, willing her tension to escape with him.

Her mother glanced after him. "Perhaps it would be better if he went home now. It was enough for him simply to be seen out in society."

She crossed her arms as a sudden chill swept over her. "I attempted to suggest that to him, but he said he would ask if he wanted to hear my opinion."

Mama nodded. "Men rarely ask for our opinions, but they often would benefit from them if they would only take the time to listen."

Abigail agreed wholeheartedly with her mother. "Has anyone asked you about the…incident or Robert's involvement?"

"No, dear. At least not overtly." Mama shifted her gaze to a passing footman and snagged a glass of champagne. "Like a fox circling the chicken coop, they are waiting for the opportune moment to strike, and I don't intend to provide them with one."

Abigail snatched a glass for herself, mostly to occupy her hands. There was no sign of Georgiana or Henrietta, so she would have to remain with her mother, who was now engaged in conversation with yet another acquaintance. She stood to the side, within Mama's view, but not listening to her conversation. She could, however, hear the discussion going on behind her.

"I can't imagine what it would be like to be betrothed to

a murderer."

Abigail tensed. She did not recognize the speaker.

"There's no way to know if he's guilty. Papa said the whole thing will likely blow over. The magistrate cannot force a peer to be questioned, and even if they find evidence that he is guilty, they are unlikely to do anything about it. She was just a maid, after all."

Abigail shifted to her other foot, suddenly sensitive to the crushing weight of dread. She could tell them exactly what it was like to be betrothed to a potential murderer. But she wouldn't, of course. A glance at Mama revealed her deep in conversation and unaware of what was being said behind her. Abigail wished she could borrow the fairy godmother from her favorite story, *Cinderella*. Perhaps the magic wand could whisk her away from here and help her find her prince.

Behind her, the conversation continued.

"But what if he is innocent? It would be terrible to be accused of something you didn't do."

"Well yes, but the papers are implying that she was his mistress. Who else could have done it?"

"Footpads? After all, she was carrying all of her possessions with her."

"But she was a maid. How many possessions could she have had? Certainly none would have been valuable."

"I suppose it is possible that someone else killed her, but don't you find it more likely that Lord Hinsdale did it in a fit of rage because she dared to leave him?"

"Well, it is possible. But unlike some other gentlemen we know, I've never seen him become angry or throw a tantrum like a child."

"He didn't seem very happy tonight."

"Would you be? Knowing everyone was watching you? Judging you? Waiting for you to do something to prove your innocence or guilt?"

Abigail risked a glance over her shoulder. It was Elinor Price who had spoken. She was a kind, sensible girl who rarely engaged in gossip of the malicious sort.

"Ladies, are you in need of an introduction?"

Abigail realized she had been holding her breath and let it out slowly. Lord Longcroft's words soothed her frazzled nerves.

"No…no, my lord," mumbled one of the girls.

"Then why are you not dancing? This is a ball, is it not?"

"Of course, my lord. We were simply enjoying refreshment."

"Off with you, then. Your glasses are empty." He waved his arm in a shooing motion.

Abigail stifled a laugh as the girl's hurried away from him.

He turned to her, a lopsided smile gracing his handsome features. "Lady Abigail, it is always a pleasure to see you." He bowed over her hand. "Would you care to join me for the next set?"

She glanced around, but could not see Robert anywhere in the ballroom.

"Of course, my lord. I thank you for the invitation." She slid her arm through his and moved onto the dance floor, wondering if her fairy godmother had taken pity on her and sent her a prince in the form of her best friend's brother.

"In addition to the excellent company, I find myself in need of an expert on ladies attire, and I always seek out the best."

"Indeed?" She bit her lip, disconcerted by the rush

of excitement his words elicited in her. "How may I be of service?"

"My mother's birthday approaches, and as she has finally decided to reenter society since Elizabeth will soon make her come out, I would like to purchase something special for her. Something that might make her feel more at ease while out in public."

Lady Longcroft had been out of society since her husband's passing more than two years prior. She had gone into mourning and had never reemerged. It was wonderful for the younger girls that their mother would be available to help them navigate their coming out. Perhaps she would even push Georgiana to accept one of the many proposals she received with alarming frequency.

Abigail narrowed her eyes. "That is a tall order." She ran through the catalogue of lady's attire and accessories in her head. "Were you thinking of jewelry, or an item of clothing?"

He inclined his head. "To be honest, I wasn't thinking of anything specific. That's where you come in."

She nodded. "Perhaps a fichu. The right one will be stylish and coordinate with most all of her gowns. It could also serve as a wrap to prevent her from catching a chill."

He nodded. "That sounds as if it could be just the thing. How do I go about choosing one?"

"Perhaps it would be best if Georgiana and I helped you make the selection." She met his gaze and raised her brows.

"Yes, I suppose that makes more sense than attempting to choose something on my own. Georgiana will also be more familiar with her wardrobe than I. When would be a convenient time for you to join us?"

For a moment Abigail allowed herself to enjoy the

image of Edmund and she out together, searching shops for the perfect gift for his mother. It was a much easier image to conjure than her doing the same with Robert. Even if Robert was willing, she didn't think it would be possible to please his mother.

"Perhaps next week? I would prefer to be out as little as possible until something else occurs to occupy the gossips."

"Yes, of course."

The warmth of his hand against her back penetrated her gown and made her want to move closer, to be held and reassured that everything would be all right, but alas, it ought to be Robert comforting her and reassuring her. She looked up at Edmund and straight into his kind brown eyes and allowed herself to imagine for a moment that he was her betrothed. She wasn't sure when she began to think of him as Edmund instead of Lord Longcroft, but it was disconcerting to acknowledge that she was much more at ease with him than she had been with Robert since he returned from the continent.

After a moment of silence, he raised a brow. "I was expecting to be commended for my bravery."

Abigail snapped out of her daydream. "I'm sorry?"

He bit back a grin. "Did you not see me dancing with Lady Needler earlier? I was certain you of all people would compliment me on my courageousness."

She couldn't prevent a giggle from escaping. "You are very brave. You might have suffered an injury. Are you certain you weren't struck?"

He choked back a laugh and leaned closer. "I believe I would have been knocked down by a direct hit."

His warm breath caressed the shell of her ear and she

shivered. There was a time when she had conversed easily with Robert, but in truth she had been uncomfortable with him even before their betrothal was made official. Perhaps she was so comfortable with Edmund because he saw her only as a friend and not a romantic interest.

She glanced around the ballroom, but there was still no sign of Robert. It was possible he had left the ball without even saying goodbye. Each time she interacted with him, she was more and more certain that she had made the right decision to break off their engagement once the murder was solved.

When the set ended, Edmund led her back to her mother. "Well, that's unfortunate."

She followed his gaze to the man standing with her mother. Lord Oakley. No doubt he hoped to quiz her for information.

Edmund squeezed her arm. "Do be careful what you say to him. He is the ringleader of those betting in the book at White's. I believe he hopes Hinsdale is guilty."

He released her arm as they reached Mama, and she felt the loss of his support. She forced her lips to form a smile. "Good evening, Lord Oakley."

"Lady Abigail, how lovely to see you." He nodded toward Edmund. "Longcroft."

"Oakley." Edmund nodded. "Lady Jaffrey, Lady Abigail, always a pleasure." He bowed, and Abigail forced herself not to watch him walk away. It wouldn't do for anyone to note her growing fondness for him.

"Lady Abigail, would you care to dance?"

"I would be honored, my lord." She allowed him to lead her to where the other dancers had gathered to wait for the next set to start. Thankfully this was a country dance, so she would not be forced to make as much mundane conversation with him as she would have had to if it had been a waltz.

He studied her face. "You seem to be handling yourself well, all things considered."

She had no idea how to respond to that. It wasn't exactly a compliment, and she didn't wish to give the impression that she doubted Robert. "Thank you, my lord."

He took her hand as the music started. "It must be difficult not knowing."

She narrowed her eyes. "I beg your pardon?"

They separated, but he kept his eyes on her as they moved down the line. He caught her gaze as they promenaded. "Doesn't it bother you not to know whether he is guilty or innocent?"

"I am certain of Robert's innocence. The only difficulty, if you must call it that, is waiting for the murderer to be identified."

Oakley's eyes widened. "You are that certain of his innocence?"

"Yes."

"I am not your enemy, you know. I simply wish to know the truth."

"Would you be so interested in the truth if you hadn't wagered on the result?"

"I concede only that I may have underestimated you."

They finished the rest of the set in near silence. He led her back to her mother and left quickly, apparently dissatisfied at not having gleaned any gossip to share, which was no doubt the purpose of his attention.

Georglana sought her out and looped an arm through

hers. She took her to an empty seating area and chose a settee that was partially blocked by a large potted palm.

"Edmund tells me that we are to go shopping."

Her face grew warm at the mention of Edmund, and she hoped Georgiana would attribute it to her recent turn on the dance floor. "Yes, he asked me to help him select a present for your mother's birthday." She picked at a thread on her glove so she wouldn't have to meet Georgiana's assessing eyes. "We had discussed fashion at the Wrexham ball, and apparently that has led him to believe that I am somewhat of an expert."

"I see."

Abigail looked up.

"It's just that Edmund has never paid any attention to fashion before, and he certainly has never attempted to purchase anything stylish for any of us." Georgiana met her stare and remained silent.

"He indicated that your mother is planning to return to society since Elizabeth is coming out, and he wanted to find something special for her, something that might bolster her confidence."

Georgiana's eyes narrowed. "How thoughtful of him." She squeezed Abigail's hand. "I'm sorry to interrogate you. It's just that if Edmund actually manages to remember one of our birthdays, he usually leaves the selection of a present to the shopkeeper."

Abigail smiled. "Perhaps the reality of having six unwed sisters is weighing on him. I'm certain he welcomes your mother's assistance in seeing you all properly settled."

"Yes, he is the kindest of brothers, if a bit absentminded. He is quite determined that Henrietta marry again, though of course she refuses."

Abigail clasped her hands. "I understand her reluctance. My current situation is nothing compared to her circumstances, but I can see why it is difficult for her to forget."

Georgiana glanced around before speaking. "I think perhaps the dilemma for both of you is that you were deceived by the men you trusted most. I imagine that makes it a challenge to trust again."

Abigail studied the parquet pattern on the floor. It was an astute observation, though not one she wanted to have to own up to. Georgiana was correct. She no longer fully trusted Robert. Or her own judgment.

Georgiana looked into her eyes. "I didn't mean to upset you. Have faith. Somehow, it will all work itself out in the end." She stood and held out her hand to Abigail. "Come, we must rejoin the party before our absence is noticed."

Abigail clasped her hand as if she was depending upon Georgiana to lead her from a burning building.

Chapter Seven

Abigail had been correct to trust her brother George with her eavesdropping scheme. He knew that if the damper was left open one could hear every word spoken in the parlor from the bedchamber above. Later on she would spend some time considering what things he may have overheard over the years, but for now she was more concerned with the Bow Street runner's visit.

She had awoken with the dawn and summoned her maid to help her dress. Her father would wish to hold the interview early so the runner would be long gone before any afternoon callers might arrive.

"I don't understand why you need to be up and about before the investigator arrives," Judith said as she pinned another section of Abigail's hair. "I thought your father refused to allow you to be interviewed."

"He did." She flinched as Judith rather painfully twisted another lock of her hair. Judith did not enjoy mornings, which was why Abigail normally didn't wake her when she rose early. She usually had Judith dress her hair in a more formal manner later in the day.

"Then why are we putting ourselves through this at such an early hour?"

Wincing as a pin scraped against her scalp, she mumbled, "I always enjoy a little bloodshed in the morning."

"What?"

"I want to be prepared in case Papa changes his mind about letting me speak with the runner. I am the one who spent the most time with Robert at the ball."

"And when have you ever known your father to change his mind?" Judith met her eyes in the mirror.

"There is always a first time for everything." Judith slipped in another pin, and Abigail popped up to prevent her from adding more. "You may go back to bed or whatever it is you would normally do at this time of the morning. I am going to the parlor." She opened a drawer in her writing desk and pulled out a seldom worked on embroidery project.

"Normal people are sleeping at this time of the morning," Judith said as she shoved Abigail's brushes and comb into a drawer. She glanced over at Abigail. "Who do you think you're going to fool with that?" Her lips curved into her first smile of the day. "You haven't worked on it in months. Maybe even years."

Abigail raised her nose and in her most proper voice said, "I have decided that is high time I return to my embroidery. It is a fitting activity for a lady."

Judith's laughter trailed after her down the corridor.

After creeping down the staircase and letting Baxter perform his morning ritual in the garden, she positioned herself inside the parlor. Her embroidery remained in her lap so if her presence was questioned, she could claim the light was better here than in her chamber. She did her best to unsnarl the yarn while keeping one ear out for the opening of the front door. The clank of metal against the cobblestones sounded and she rushed to the window, but it was just someone passing by, likely on his way to the park to exercise his horse. She resumed her position on the settee and placed a few stitches before quickly growing bored.

Finally, the front door creaked open and the indiscernible murmur of voices travelled down the corridor. She stiffened, waiting to determine the location of the interview. "… his lordship awaits you in his study." Williams' faint words carried to the parlor.

Damn and blast. She leapt from the settee and softly shut the parlor door on a heartbroken Baxter. She couldn't risk him exposing her hiding place outside Papa's study. After looking in both directions to make sure no one was about, she crept down the corridor, stepping as lightly as possible while still maintaining a normal walking pattern in case she was spotted. She sped through the servant's corridor and crouched next to the door to Papa's study. Last night she had come down and left the door slightly ajar, correctly guessing that no one would notice since the door was all but hidden in the corner next to a large bookcase. It was used primarily to remove ash from the fireplace without having to track it through the public areas of the house.

Her back against the wall, she leaned against the doorframe but could not make out what was being said. Their voices became more distinct as they moved toward Papa's desk at the back of the chamber.

"Lord Jaffrey, thank you for agreeing to meet with me today. Your cooperation is appreciated."

Chairs scraped against the floor and Papa spoke. "I'm not sure I have any information that will aid your investigation."

"You attended a ball at Wrexham House the night Sarah Davies disappeared. Is that correct?" the runner asked.

"Yes."

"About what time did you arrive?"

"As you know, my daughter is engaged to Lord Wrexham's son, Lord Hinsdale. The ball was being held in their honor, so naturally we arrived early, before most of the guests began to appear."

"And was Lord Hinsdale present when you arrived?"

"Yes. He and my daughter opened the dancing."

Papers shuffled and the runner spoke again. Abigail tuned out as he asked more mundane questions with obvious answers. However, the next question caught her attention.

"At the time that you gave your permission for your daughter to marry, were you aware that Lord Hinsdale had a mistress?"

"We did not discuss it, as it was not material to the marriage settlements. As I'm sure you are aware, it is common for men to keep a mistress, and that is no one's business but their own."

"Do you have a mistress, Lord Jaffrey?"

"That is irrelevant to your purpose in questioning me today."

Abigail's pulse thundered. How did the runner dare speak to her father like that?

"Does it bother you that your daughter's betrothed had a mistress?"

"Again, my opinion on that matter is immaterial to your

investigation. Do you have any other questions?"

"Do you recall where Lord Hinsdale was around midnight on the night of the ball?"

"I do not."

"Can you tell me when you did see him?"

"We spoke upon our arrival at Wrexham House. I watched him dance with my daughter, and I don't believe I saw him again until after midnight when he apologized to Abigail for his absence and stated that his sister's maid was missing."

"Are you certain it was after midnight when this conversation took place?"

"Yes."

"So Lord Hinsdale was unaccounted for from the time of the first dance until sometime after midnight. Is that correct?"

"I cannot speak for anyone else, but I was unaware of his whereabouts during that time."

Abigail was impressed with the way Papa carefully worded his responses so as to not give away any information that wasn't specifically requested. Though of course, the investigator had been hired to prove Robert's innocence, so his caution might have been a bit overzealous.

"Did your daughter see or speak with Lord Hinsdale between the end of their dance and the time that he returned to the ballroom to announce that the maid was missing?"

"Not that I am aware of. She asked me if I had seen him, and I went searching for him in the card room."

"But you did not find him there?"

"No."

"Did you look for him anywhere else?"

"There wasn't any place else to look. I spoke with Lord Wrexham, but he told me he did not know where his son was."

"I see," said the magistrate.

"You have been to Wrexham House, I presume. It is a rather large place. There were people in the ballroom, on the terrace, in the card room, the billiard room, the conservatory—it would not be unheard of for it to be difficult to locate someone in the crush. I once spent nearly an hour trying to locate my own wife at a ball."

Someone touched her shoulder and Abigail stifled a scream and banged her hand against the door, causing it to slam closed. Her heart thundered in her ears as she dove behind the door and whipped around to see who had found her out. A happy Baxter trotted over, his nails clicking against the wood floor, and licked Abigail's face as Judith stared down at her, her hands on her hips.

Footsteps sounded from the study and her father appeared in the doorway.

"What in heaven's name is going on out here?"

"My apologies for the disturbance, my lord," said Judith. "Baxter was not interested in having his bath this morning and made a run for it."

"I wish I could make a run for it," Papa mumbled. "Very well, carry on."

He went back into the study and closed the door firmly. If he had any notion that Abigail was behind the door, he didn't let on.

Judith grabbed her elbow and towed her down the corridor. "I knew you were up to no good. I found poor Baxter trapped in the parlor. As soon as I released him he led me to you." She shook her head. "The embroidery ought to have tipped me off."

"Judith! My father is meeting with the runner, and I must know what's happening with the investigation. After all, Robert is my fiancé."

"You should not spy on your father. You could have been caught."

"I was in no danger of being caught until you showed up. I need to know if Robert is innocent."

She shook her head. "You'll have to wait for the magistrate's report for that."

"Perhaps, but I cannot rely on the magistrate to do a thorough investigation. You know as well as I do that unless there is irrefutable proof that Robert is guilty, he will not be charged."

Judith raised her brows. "It's entirely possible that even if he is guilty he won't be charged."

Abigail turned to her and took her hand. "If it had been you, you know I would not give up until I found out who did it. Sarah deserves that as well."

Judith squeezed her hand and wiped at her eyes. "That is neither here nor there."

She and Baxter returned to the parlor. Having given up on the embroidery, she pulled out her sketch book and attempted to finish her latest design while she waited for Papa to finish speaking with the runner. She hadn't realized he had left until Papa poked his head into the parlor. "Come with me."

She jumped up and followed him toward his study, anxious to find out if the runner revealed any useful information after Judith had dragged her away. Her stomach flitted about in anticipation. He closed the door behind her and waved to the armchairs set in front of the fireplace.

"Eavesdropping on the runner was a dangerous ploy. If he had known you were out there, he might have demanded an audience with you."

She clasped her hands as heat surged up her neck and suffused her cheeks. "I'm sorry, Papa, but *I* am the one who is engaged to Robert. I deserve to know what is happening with the investigation."

"Be that as it may, you will follow my orders in the future. I do not want you involved in any way with the investigation."

"Yes, Papa." Her pulse slowed as his expression softened.

He sat in the chair across from her and steepled his fingers. "How much did you hear?"

"I heard everything up until Judith scared me and I hit the door."

He smiled. "Ah, so that's what happened. Not that I could have missed the clicking of Baxter's claws on the floor. Wherever you go, he goes."

Abigail stroked Baxter's head.

"In short, though the runner hasn't been able to identify any other suspects, he also hasn't found any evidence that points to Robert. So the investigation continues."

She slid down to the floor and put her head on her father's lap. "Papa, what if they never determine who murdered her?"

"That is a very real possibility," he said as he stroked her hair.

She sucked in a ragged breath. "I could not go through with the marriage without knowing. I'd always wonder if he's guilty."

"Abigail, I understand that you are upset, but you made

a commitment to Robert and you cannot abandon him now."

"But Papa, Robert showed me the note the maid wrote to him. They had been together for some time, and she thought he was going to marry her." She wiped at the tears streaming from her eyes. "He admitted that he loved her. How can I marry a man who loves someone else, even if she is gone?"

He placed a finger under her chin and pushed gently so she sat up and met his eyes. He took out his handkerchief and wiped her tears. "Darling, Lord Wrexham is one of my oldest friends. We were at Eton together. We cannot abandon his family in their time of need. If evidence is found implicating Robert in the murder, I will allow you to break your engagement. But for now, the Wrexham family needs our support."

Her heart sank, trapped as surely as if it had been caged by her own integrity. She would wait for the outcome of the investigation before acting, but the more she considered her options, the more certain she became that she would live out her life alone, for surely no one else would want her. While standing by Robert might be the virtuous choice, it had narrowed her options to marriage to Robert or spinsterhood.

"Yes, Papa. I understand."

He stood and pulled her into a hug. "That's my girl."

Abigail left her father and returned to her bedchamber to repair her appearance. She wet a length of toweling and pressed it over her eyes, hoping to remove the puffiness her tears had created. She had been too busy to visit Robert's sister, Lady Jane, but today she would make time to see her.

Chapter Eight

Abigail waited impatiently for Jane to join her in the morning room at Wrexham House. The butler, who normally kept his countenance carefully schooled, seemed astonished to see her. As she paced, she glanced out the window. Mama had insisted on dropping Abigail off on the way to her appointment because she was certain it was going to rain. So far, the sun continued to shine brightly in the sky.

Soft footsteps heralded the arrival of Jane. Finally.

"Abigail." Jane rushed into her arms.

"Why are you wearing your cloak?" Abigail asked.

"Though I'm thrilled to see you, I am due at Longcroft to visit with Lady Elizabeth." She pulled back to study Abigail's face. "You only found me at home because I've been delayed while Mama decides who is available to accompany me."

"I will go with you. Is Robert available to take us?"

Jane's eyes crinkled. "I don't know, but I'd rather not

wait for someone to summon him and have to wait for him to arrive."

"I don't understand."

"Oh, don't you know? Robert doesn't live here anymore."

Her stomach plunged. "What? Since when?"

Jane waved her hand in the air. "Oh, he secured his own quarters more than a fortnight ago."

And he hadn't said anything to Abigail. If Jane's timing was correct, he hadn't been living here when the ball was held. That could explain why he had been chasing after his mistress before the ball. Abigail focused on Jane, who was studying her closely.

"Is the carriage available? Perhaps your mother would allow us to take the short trip ourselves?"

"Perhaps. I'll go find out," she called over her shoulder as she entered the corridor.

Abigail turned back to the window and watched a goldfinch flit from a bush to a tree, enjoying its freedom. After discovering that Robert had yet another secret he had kept from her, she realized she identified more with the bird her aunt kept in a cage in her parlor. Trapped in a situation over which she had little control. What if she had needed to contact him? His behavior was becoming more and more erratic with each passing day. Was it just pressure from the investigation pressing on him, or the weight of guilt?

Jane bustled back into the room and Abigail turned from the window.

"Mama is having the carriage readied for us, so we have a few minutes to talk. Did you come for a reason?"

Jane sat and Abigail took the chair next to her. "I have been wanting to visit for some time, to see how you're coping with everything that's happened."

Jane's face paled. "Sarah wasn't just my maid. She was also my friend. Losing her was devastating."

Abigail took her hand. "How are you faring with your new maid?"

Jane scrunched her nose. "We are managing, but Mary isn't nearly as talented as Sarah was. She was very interested in fashion, so she helped me choose my gowns and had great skill with hair. That's why Mama hired her instead of giving the position to Mary."

"Who is Mary?"

"She is now my lady's maid, but she has been on our staff for several years, working as a chamber maid."

Interesting. Abigail wondered if she might have resented Sarah for being hired for the job she coveted. Being a lady's maid was quite a step up from chamber maid. "Did Mary leave the house the night of the ball?"

"Not that I am aware. You know that Mama didn't allow me to attend the ball, so I was in my bedchamber for most of the evening."

Abigail bit back a sigh. It seemed unlikely that a woman would have been able to strangle Sarah, anyway.

"I did know that Sarah was leaving that night, and I didn't share her secret with anyone. I helped her pack her things."

"Did she take all of her belongings with her?"

"Yes. But she wouldn't tell me where she was going. She didn't want Robert to find out. I blame him for pushing her away."

Abigail froze. Though she needed to tread lightly, she had to know if Jane at all suspected Robert. "Do you know if Robert left the house that night?"

"He came to me as soon as the footman delivered Sarah's note. He begged me to tell him where she had gone, but I refused. I don't know what he did after he left my chamber." She clasped Abigail's wrist. "You don't think he killed Sarah, do you?"

"I don't want to believe that, but I'm not sure what to think anymore."

"Abigail, Robert didn't kill Sarah. I'm sure of it. He was frantic to find her, but he would not have hurt her."

She wasn't sure whether that made her feel better or worse. He said he loved Sarah, but he had never given any indication that he felt the same way about her, the woman who was to be his wife.

She stood and paced to the window. The goldfinch was still there, happily moving from tree to tree. "Jane, how did the other staff members feel about Sarah?"

"I believe she was well liked."

"Was there anyone in particular who maybe liked her more than he should have? One of the male servants?"

"She did say once that one of the grooms made her nervous, but she didn't want to tell me which one because she didn't want to get him in trouble. And Thomas, one of the footmen, was very friendly with her, but she never said a bad word about him."

Just then, the butler appeared in the doorway. "The carriage awaits, my lady."

"Thank you, Hobbs. We'll be with you shortly." The butler left, and Jane came to stand next to her. "Do you think once you and Robert are married, you could convince Mama not to delay my come out? She thinks that I should wait another year until the gossip over the murder dies down."

"I doubt she would appreciate me expressing my opinion."

"On the contrary, Mama respects your opinion greatly. She constantly offers you up as an example of what my behavior should be."

How extraordinary. If someone had asked, Abigail would have said that Lady Wrexham barely tolerated her.

"I'll see what I can do to convince your mother not to delay your come out," she said to Jane, unable to make any other promises. "I'm sure Elizabeth is expecting you, so we'd best head for the carriage."

As they drew near to the front door, the butler approached her. "Lady Abigail, this was delivered for you a few moments ago."

"Thank you." Her name was on the front of the missive, but she didn't recognize the handwriting. "Can you tell me who delivered it?"

"I'm afraid not, my lady. It was handed to one of the grooms outside with the carriage. Very improper, I must say."

If the butler hadn't recognized the messenger, then it was likely the groom didn't either, so there was no point in raising anyone's curiosity by questioning the groom.

Abigail sat across from Jane in the carriage and opened the note.

Do not marry Lord Hinsdale. He cannot be trusted.

Her head buzzed with the rush of blood surging past her temples.

"Abigail, what is it?" Jane asked in a high, nervous voice.

She sucked in a deep breath and willed her voice to remain steady. "It's nothing. Just a note from my mother reminding me to send for the carriage when I'm ready to go home."

Jane met and held her eyes, but didn't ask any more questions.

• • •

A knock sounded and Edmund glanced up from his calculations. He was very close to determining the exact thickness of the glass needed for the greenhouse, and he did not welcome the interruption. Hoping to save some money on the project, he had devised a plan to use different thicknesses of glass for the panes depending on their location and amount of wind resistance required, and he was nearly finished with the computations. He sighed and pushed his papers aside. "Enter."

Woolford bowed. "My lord, Lady Abigail is here. If I may say, she appears a bit undone."

Hell and damnation. Georgiana and Henrietta were off visiting someone. It wasn't proper for him to meet alone with Abigail, but he couldn't turn her away, and he could not have his mother or one of his younger sister's serve as chaperon because he did not want them to be privy to their concerns about the murder. There could be no other reason for her to appear on his doorstep unannounced.

"Please show her to the morning room, Woolford. And have tea sent."

"Very well, my lord."

He paced about his study for a few moments before

deeming adequate time had passed for Abigail to settle in the morning room. Not knowing what had upset her made him uneasy. No doubt it had something to do with Hinsdale.

Since the last thing he wanted was to startle her, he walked down the corridor as noisily as possible. She glanced up and met his eyes just as he stepped through the doorway and for one startling moment he wished he could take her in his arms and soothe her worries. But of course it wasn't his place to do that. "I'm afraid Georgiana and Henrietta are not available."

Abigail nodded. "Woolford told me as much, but I needed to speak with someone."

He sat across from her. "I am at your disposal."

Instead of speaking, she handed him a note. Their fingers brushed as he took it from her and electricity pulsed through him. Instead of dwelling on the sensation, he studied the missive. It didn't take long to read. Anger surged through him.

"Who delivered this?"

"I don't know. Lord Wrexham's butler gave it to me after it was handed to a groom in front of the house. No one seems to know where it came from."

The situation was going from bad to worse. He ran his fingers through his hair.

"I figured it wouldn't do any good to interview the groom or press the butler further. If either of them had recognized the person who delivered the note, they would have said so."

"Yes, I suppose you are correct."

Edmund studied the worry lines that had formed around her eyes and mouth. He disliked seeing her in such a state. He wasn't sure when she had transformed from his little sister's friend into a woman, but he was very aware of her now. Small tendrils of her auburn hair had come loose and curled against her cheeks, making him want to brush them aside. It bothered him to see her lovely visage so troubled, and he wished he could find a way to bring the light back to her eyes. Damn Hinsdale for putting her through this.

"Do you mind if I pour the tea?" she asked after a maid set the tray between them.

"Of course not. I'm certain you are more equal to the task than I."

Once she had fixed tea for them both, she said, "I do have some other information to share. I called on Lady Jane this morning for the first time since the murder. She said that her maid was generally well liked among the staff. There was a groom who made her uneasy, and also a footman with whom she was friendly, both of whom openly admired her."

"That is much the same report that Woolford received from his cousin, and likely the closest we will come to a suspect list. I will make sure the runner Lord Wrexham hired investigates both men."

Abigail set down her tea and clasped her hands together. "There is more. Sarah, the maid who was…died, was hired from outside the household." She took a deep breath before continuing. "Jane's new maid is the one who was passed over for the position."

"Ah, so there could be some resentment on her part."

"Perhaps, though Jane did say she didn't think her new maid left the house on the night of the murder."

"Still, it's worth looking into."

She nodded. "Jane also shared that Robert moved out of Wrexham House several weeks ago, so he was not living there at the time of the murder."

Edmund had no idea how to respond to that. He lifted his hand and almost placed it over hers, then returned it to his lap. He shouldn't even be here alone with her, let alone touching her, but she was so forlorn he wished he knew of a way to assuage her pain.

After clearing his throat, he said, "Since he attended the ball the evening of the murder, I don't believe that his housing is relevant to the investigation. We may have to accept that the murder may never be solved."

She closed her eyes briefly before responding. "Yes, I've been prepared for that from the beginning."

He took a sip of tea, waiting in the hope that she might say more. "Woolford's cousin said the maid's family is not completely without means, so they're unlikely to let the case drop without some sort of resolution."

Her eyes narrowed. "Though surely Lord Wrexham has more influence, and money, than the girl's family."

"Yes, of course, but he is pushing for a resolution as well. Though we both know it is unlikely that they would ever declare Hinsdale guilty regardless of the evidence, Wrexham wants his son declared innocent as much as the girl's family wants the murderer found."

Abigail focused on her tea, stirring in another lump of sugar and taking a sip. "So where do we go from here?"

"We investigate the three servants Jane and Woolford identified, and also determine who sent you that note."

He glanced at Abigail, who after nodding briefly, remained unnaturally still in her chair. Perhaps it had been a mistake to have this discussion with her. Georgiana was always underfoot, and the one time he needed her, she was nowhere to be found.

Finally, Abigail looked up and met his eyes. "We mustn't forget Robert. He is still a suspect."

"Pardon my frankness, but it seems unlikely that he would have chased after the girl to kill her. Perhaps he could have strangled her in a fit of rage, but following her from the house would have given him sufficient time to cool down before confronting her. And he doesn't seem the type to get his hands dirty."

"I don't believe Robert was absent from the ball long enough to commit the m…murder." Abigail forced the words out, and again he started to reach for her hand before remembering himself.

"He said she had already left by the time he received her note. Though he could have ordered someone else to find her."

"If he did, neither he nor his messenger is likely to admit to it." Edmund tapped his index finger against the top of the table. It was unlikely that an official determination would be released anytime soon. He needed to make time to go to White's again and see which way the gossip was leaning. And also check the betting book, which had proved to be surprisingly accurate with this sort of wager.

"I'm sorry to ask you this, but did Robert's relationship with the maid end after your betrothal was announced?" Her face flushed and he regretted his question immediately.

"I…I'm not sure. I believe from what he said that he was trying to convince her to stay on as his mistress."

Managing one woman was difficult enough. Why would any sane man want to juggle two? Especially when one of them was Abigail. Her beauty shined even through her anguish. If he were about to marry a woman like her, he certainly wouldn't have any desire for a mistress.

"Robert showed me the letter Sarah had had a footman deliver to him just after she ran away. It said that she loved him, but she would not stay with him unless he could offer her marriage."

He had to bite his tongue to stop himself from asking what had motivated Abigail to accept an offer from a dolt like Hinsdale in the first place. "Did he share it with the authorities?"

"That is what he told me. But clearly he did not let them keep it."

Hinsdale must have had feelings for the girl, then. Perhaps he was only guilty of being stupid and selfish, but not murder. Regardless, Edmund's loyalties were with Abigail. Who would want to enter into a marriage knowing from the beginning that your betrothed was enamored with someone else? An unexpected urge to take her into his arms and comfort her nearly overwhelmed him. He cupped his palm over her cheek and pushed gently until she met his eyes, but before he could think of something comforting to say, Georgiana's voice carried down the corridor and he leapt from his chair.

It was not his place to comfort her. He had to solve the mystery and assure his sisters, and himself, that Abigail would be safe with Hinsdale.

Chapter Nine

Edmund continued to stare unseeingly out the window as the ladies chatted behind him. He despised this situation in which Hinsdale had placed Abigail. Numbers and logic were his forte, not veiled clues and intrigue. It really wasn't his place to become involved, yet he would not renege on the promise he had made to help Abigail.

The room grew quiet.

"I should be heading home," Abigail said.

Georgiana popped up and rang the bell. "I'll have Woolford fetch Judith."

"I'm afraid Judith isn't here. My mother dropped me off at Wrexham House, and Lady Jane brought me here in her carriage."

Georgiana turned to stare at him, and he spoke to cut her off. "I will take you home," he said.

"There is no need, my lord. It is but a short distance away."

He crossed his arms. "I disagree. We must assure your

safety, and if anyone attempts to deliver another note to you, we must detain him so we can question him to determine who is behind the scheme and why." He met her eyes and said more softly, "It could lead us to the killer."

Abigail looked away. "If you insist, my lord. I appreciate your concern."

"I do insist."

Georgiana gave him an appraising look. "Thank you, Edmund. I would join you, but Hen and I promised to help mother with something."

They moved into the corridor and he took Abigail's cloak from Woolford and gently placed it over her delicate frame, then they exited out the door.

It had been sunny earlier, but as if the weather had somehow sensed his mood, dark clouds formed on the horizon, promising rain. "Woolford, I don't like the look of that sky. Have them ready the curricle and bring it around."

He left to issue the order, and Edmund turned back to Abigail. "I would like to ask something of you."

"Of course, my lord."

"You must promise me that you will not go out again without male escort of some sort. At the very least have a footman accompany you."

Her green eyes finally came to life, and he knew from experience with his sisters that she was about to argue. At least it had snapped her out of her melancholy.

"But what if someone is sent to deliver another note but is too afraid to approach me when others are present? We might miss out on information important to our investigation."

He took both of her hands in his, the heat from her transferring through the layers of both of their gloves.

She leaned slightly toward him and suddenly his breeches seemed too small. "Hang the investigation. Your safety is the most important thing."

Abigail's face flushed.

He ran his thumbs across her knuckles. "Promise me you will not leave your house unescorted."

She dragged in an unsteady breath. "Yes, my lord."

"Very well." He kept hold of her left hand as his curricle came around the corner of the house, and continued to hold it until Abigail was safely in her seat. He moved quickly around to the other side and sat next to her. After picking up the reins and clucking the horses into motion, he asked, "You will to talk to your father about the note as soon as you arrive?"

She nodded. "I would not keep this from Papa. I suspect he will tell me the same thing you did and I shall no longer have any freedom to move about at my own will."

Though he didn't envy her position, he delighted in the fire that had returned to her voice. "Take heart. This will soon pass and you can resume your normal life."

"I'm not sure I know what my normal life is supposed to be anymore."

Damn his quick tongue. He seemed to have a knack for steering their conversations in the wrong direction. But since he had, he might as well ask the question that had been plaguing him. "Once again I must beg your forgiveness for my impertinence, but I wish to know if you think Hinsdale is guilty of murder."

"You are not impertinent. You have helped me more than you will know, and for that I am grateful." She paused. "I do not believe that Robert killed Sarah. Unfortunately, I also don't believe that he is the man I had assumed he was."

Her open admission surprised him, but it likely had more to do with her growing distrust of Hinsdale than anything to do with him. He stopped the curricle in front of her house.

"Thank you for bringing me home, my lord."

"It was my pleasure." He secured the reins and moved around to hand her down. Her hand fit so well inside his, as if had been designed for that purpose. "I shall look forward to our shopping expedition on Friday."

She managed a genuine smile for him. "As will I."

• • •

White's was busier than he had expected. Much to his chagrin, Edmund would have to forgo his usual habit of avoiding people and instead covertly seek information. He stopped first at the betting book and discretely paged through the recent bets to locate the wagers about Hinsdale.

He suppressed a snort. *Lord Alvanley bets Mr. Goddard five pounds that Mr. G. Talbot does not die a natural death.* Unless he was planning to kill the man himself, he might have to wait a bit to collect on that wager.

Mr. Talbot bets a certain gentleman a certain sum, that a certain event does not take place within a certain time. These types of wagers were exactly why Edmund never participated. He saw no reason to throw money to the wind.

Finally, he came across the active wagers for and against Hinsdale's innocence. The overwhelming majority backed his innocence, but the murderer would have to be officially identified in order for the bet to pay out either way. And for Lady Abigail to learn whether her future husband was a killer.

There were also several wagers as to whether Lady Abigail would break off her engagement to Hinsdale. The odds were three to one that she would. Surely no one could blame her if she did. He suspected the only reason she hadn't already was because of her father's long-standing friendship with Wrexham.

The next two wagers made him angry. And thankful that ladies were not allowed in White's. He pulled at his now vise-like collar. The odds were twenty to one that *No one will make an offer for Lady A. if she breaks her betrothal to Lord H.* Worse yet, a similar bet had odds at thirty to one that she would end up a spinster. She was an innocent victim of this mess, and yet she stood to lose the most.

"Surely you're not making a wager."

He glanced over his shoulder at Oakley. "Of course not, but I do like to follow the more interesting bets."

"Yes, Alvanley and Talbot do keep things exciting." He moved to look at the current page. "Well, that's insulting."

"Indeed." It was the most sensible thing he'd heard from Oakley in a long time. Though Edmund's preference was still to go find a dark corner in which to hide, that would not suit his purpose in being here, which was to do everything in his power to ensure Abigail's safety. The best way to discover the current gossip was to join one of the ongoing card games. Whist was his favorite because it was easy enough to win by determining which cards each player held based on the cards played.

"Oakley, would you care for a game of whist?"

He crossed his arms and leaned against the wall, grinning. "Who are you and what have you done with Longcroft?"

He raised a brow. "How can I pass up the chance to partner with you? There are few others I consider worthy." That had been a bit of a stretch, but Oakley seemed to think him sincere.

He straightened. "In that case, who are your intended victims?"

"Whoever we can find." He followed Oakley to the card room and they were soon seated with Mr. Higgins and Viscount Lanford.

"What's the wager?" Higgins asked.

Edmund shifted his gaze across the table to Oakley and raised his brows.

"A pound?" Oakley offered.

"C'mon now. Surely we can go higher than that," said Lanford.

"We could, but we find we derive our pleasure from winning, so the wager is rather irrelevant." Oakley leveled them with a look and neither of the other gentlemen commented further.

Lanford served as the dealer for the first round. When he gave a nod, Edmund cut the deck and Lanford dealt the cards. Just as he turned the last card face up to reveal hearts, Hinsdale himself entered the card room and went straight to the hazard tables.

He was more than a bit rough around the edges. In fact, he looked as if he had been up all night and hadn't bothered to change his clothing. His eyes were red-rimmed and bloodshot, and his hair stood up from his head as if he had spent the morning running his fingers through it. If he had hoped showing his face here would cut down on speculation about his guilt, he wasn't doing himself any favors by appearing at the club like that.

Edmund kept one eye on the whist table, and one eye on Hinsdale, who was involved in a high stakes round of hazard. He and Oakley won with very little effort after two rounds of play. Hinsdale, however, had not fared so well. He owed upwards of thirty pounds.

Edmund went toward Hinsdale's table and waited for the round to end. When it did, he approached the man. "May I have a word with you?"

He looked up at Edmund, clearly well into his cups. "I believe you just had ten of them."

Good lord. If he was too far into his cups to count properly, he had no hope of winning.

"If you please." He held his arm toward an empty corner in the back of the room.

Hinsdale shook his head. "I do not please."

"Truer words have never been spoken." He considered moving the man bodily, but was afraid he would resist and cause even more of a scene. He leaned down and spoke into his ear. "You're drunk and losing money hand over fist. Even if you don't give a hang about your own reputation, have a care for that of Lady Abigail and your family."

"What do you know of Lady Abigail?"

He crossed his arms and looked down on him. "She is my sister's dearest friend."

"Toss off, Longcroft."

That was it. He grabbed him by the elbow, yanked him from his chair, and dragged him into the corner. "You are making a fool of yourself, your family, and your future wife. I will have my curricle brought round and drive you home. Settle up and meet me outside."

Hinsdale opened his mouth to protest, but he cut him

off. "Follow my instructions or I will haul you out." Edmund took a deep breath and waved to a passing footman. One way or the other, Hinsdale was leaving with him.

Surprisingly, Hinsdale joined him just as his curricle came to a halt at the front entrance. Edmund climbed in and took the reins, leaving Hinsdale to find his own way up.

The streets were clogged with early evening traffic. Once Hinsdale managed to climb up, he urged the horses into a slow trot.

"You've never paid me any heed before. Why now?" he asked.

Edmund glanced over at him. There was a bit of a green tinge to him, but he had tamped down his hair and retied his cravat. "It certainly wasn't out of concern for you. I told you earlier. Lady Abigail is my sister's dearest friend. Your actions reflect upon her, as well as your family. Don't you have enough to worry about without making a spectacle of yourself at White's?"

Hinsdale glared at him but didn't respond.

A silent ride was fine with Edmund.

Edmund belatedly remembered that Hinsdale didn't live at Wrexham House anymore. He turned to Robert and found him slumped over, asleep. His deep slumber had undoubtedly been assisted by the large amount of alcohol he had consumed. Since he had no idea where his new lodgings were, he took him to Wrexham House.

The front door opened as he pulled to a stop and a footman moved to hold the horses. Edmund climbed the stairs and came face to face with Lord Wrexham, who held out his hand. "Lord Longcroft. To what do I owe the pleasure of your visit?"

"We happened to be leaving at the same time and Lord Hinsdale needed a ride home from White's," he said simply, deciding that Wrexham could deduce the circumstances on his own.

Wrexham gave his butler a look, and soon two footmen appeared and went to remove Hinsdale from Edmund's curricle. They stood shoulder to shoulder, neither looking at the other.

"He doesn't live here anymore, you know," Wrexham said. "Took his own quarters over on Bury Street a while back. But it's just as well you brought him here since he doesn't keep live in staff."

"Excellent," Edmund replied, unsure what else to say.

"He's had a rough time of it lately, as I'm sure you can imagine. Thank you for looking out for him."

"It was my pleasure." They shook hands again and Edmund took his leave. As the horses made their way through the evening traffic, he wondered if Hinsdale's decision to move out had coincided with the start of his relationship with his sister's maid. Though a lady's maid must always be available at a moment's notice, so it would have been difficult for her to leave Wrexham House without it being noted. Perhaps it was his pending nuptials that had prompted the move, but surely he intended to find a more suitable place for Lady Abigail. It was really none of his affair, but he didn't like to think of her holed up in bachelor's quarters. She deserved more.

Chapter Ten

During a long, sleepless night, Abigail resolved to change her outlook. She could not continue to mope about indefinitely, allowing circumstances to dictate her actions. No matter her situation, she resolved to be happy, to make the most of what she had, and to stop worrying about what she didn't have. It was not possible to make an informed decision about her future until the murder investigation was closed and she broke her engagement, so there was no point in spending the bulk of her time worrying over it. After all, unlike Sarah, she was lucky to still have a future.

Content with her new resolutions, Abigail exited the house into a gorgeous, sunny afternoon. After conspiring with the housekeeper that morning, she had decided to head out to buy new fabric for their staff. They would surprise the maids with new dresses, which she would help to sew. Anything that would divert her mind was a welcome occupation, and given her lack of sewing skills, much concentration would be required for her to make a serviceable dress. She waited outside for Judith to fetch a footman to accompany them.

A street urchin approached her. He couldn't have been more than six or seven, and was cleaner than she would have expected, with well-worn but not shabby clothing. She loosened her reticule to look for pennies.

"'Cuse me, milady. This is for you." He handed her a folded paper and spun away.

Nothing was written on the outside. "Wait," she called to the boy, who was already running.

He stopped and glanced over his shoulder at her, the look in his eyes like Baxter when he was caught stealing food.

"Who gave this to you?"

"A man in a uniform. He gave me a shilling to wait outside this house and give it to the young lady if she came out."

Could he be confusing a footman or groom's livery with a uniform?

At the sound of footsteps, the boy ran off. After glancing at Judith, Abigail unfolded the note. An icy chill spread over her like a blanket as she read.

You are in danger. Trust no one.

It was not signed and she didn't recognize the writing. There was no seal, and nothing noteworthy about the paper itself.

Judith peered over her shoulder. "What is that?"

Abigail refolded the note and stuffed it into her reticule. "It's nothing." Making a rapid decision, she added, "I'm afraid I need to make a quick stop at Longcroft Hall before we commence our shopping. I won't be long."

They covered the short distance in silence.

Woolford took her cloak and led Abigail to the drawing room. As she approached, Georgiana pulled her down next to her on the settee. "I thought you were shopping for fabric today."

"I am, but I needed to show you this first." She handed Georgiana the note.

She read it and looked up to meet Abigail's eyes. "Where did this come from?"

"A little boy handed it to me when I left the house." Georgiana leapt from the settee and rushed to the door. "Wait one moment. There's no point in having to repeat yourself." She opened the door and stuck her head out into the corridor. "Woolford, please ask his lordship to join us immediately."

She slammed the door and rushed back to the settee. Georgiana took her hand, which she was thankful had only a slight tremor. They didn't have long to wait.

Edmund entered the room, his eyes examining Abigail as if searching for injuries. His gaze heated her skin and her heart beat so vociferously she feared Georgiana might hear it.

"Woolford said I was needed at once. What has happened?" His eyes flitted between them.

Georgiana stood and handed him the note. "This was given to Abigail as she left her house."

He met Abigail's eyes. "Who gave this to you?"

"A little boy." She waved one hand in the air, as if it would somehow help the words escape her mouth. "It was a boy of about six or seven. At first I thought he was a street urchin, but in retrospect, he was clean and his clothes were relatively well-kept. He said a man in a uniform gave him a shilling to wait outside and deliver the note to me."

His eyes narrowed. "What type of uniform?"

Abigail sighed. "He ran off before I could ask."

Edmund sat down heavily in the armchair across from them, his eyes lined with obvious concern for her, someone he should never have had to worry over. "He may have meant a military uniform, or even a servant's livery, such as a footman or groom. There's no way to know." He scrubbed his hand across his face.

"Why would someone in the military send Abigail a note like this?" Georgiana asked.

"I don't know." He stood and paced to the window. "I think it's more likely that it came from a servant at Wrexham House, but of course there's no way to know for sure."

He turned to Abigail. "Do you recognize the writing?"

She shook her head.

"I think you should give the note to the magistrate," said Georgiana.

"I shall have to discuss it with Papa when I return home. He gave the first note to Lord Wrexham's Bow Street runner, but I'm not sure what good it may have done."

"Though it's unlikely, they might be able to match the handwriting to someone in the Wrexham household. Or at least check it against those who are under suspicion," Edmund said.

Abigail thought for a moment. "What if we're looking at this the wrong way? It could be someone who is trying to make the footman or groom look guilty. Or Robert, for that matter."

Edmund nodded. "The possibility is still open that the

murder was committed by a stranger who only wanted the maid's valuables." He glanced at Georgiana and Abigail. "Much has been written about the case in the newspapers and the scandal sheets. Whoever did it might have a clever scheme to place the blame on someone else, or maybe even hope to collect a reward for giving false clues."

Abigail blew out a breath. "We seem to be moving backward instead of forward. This is an impossible situation."

Edmund leaned forward and clasped her hand, his grip warm and strong and comforting. More comforting than it ought to have been for a man who had no formal ties to her. "It might seem that way now, but eventually the person sending the notes is going to trip up and reveal something that will help us identify him." He read the words again. "I think it's clear that whoever sent the note believes Robert is guilty."

"Or wants Abigail to believe he is guilty," Georgiana added. Her gaze paused momentarily on their clasped hands before lifting to meet Abigail's eyes. "There is no way to know if it is a warning or a threat."

And that was the biggest problem of all.

• • •

After a long day of shopping, Abigail was ready to go to bed, but first, she needed to speak with Papa about the second note.

She gave the door to his study a quick knock, then opened it. He looked up and waved her in.

"Papa, I received another note today." She placed it in front of him and sat in the chair in front of his desk.

He popped out of his chair. "Where? When?"

She explained everything quickly, bracing herself for his response.

"You must be more careful. Do not go outside without a footman or other suitable escort."

"But Papa, the child was not going to hurt me."

"Perhaps not, but the person who sent him was likely in the area. What if the child had only been a distraction so the killer could get to you?"

A jolt of icy terror slid up her spine. "Very well, Papa. I will not go outside alone. Do you still have the first note?"

"No, I gave it to the runner."

That was what she had thought. Abigail reread the note from today. "I can't be sure, but the writing looks different to me."

"I agree." He leaned back in his chair. "It seems that we are dealing with more than one person, and only one of them can be guilty of the murder."

"So, the question is, what does the other person hope to accomplish?"

"Perhaps to extort money from Wrexham or me. To scare you. To help you find the murderer. There are many possibilities." He picked up the note and placed it in the inside pocket of his coat. "I'm going to take this to the runner tonight."

She glanced up to gauge his mood, but decided it didn't matter. "Papa, there is something else."

"Yes?"

"I have not changed my mind about ending the betrothal."

He took off his glasses and rubbed his forehead. "Do you think Robert killed the girl?"

"No. I don't believe him guilty of murder, but I also no

longer believe him to be the same person I once knew him to be."

"Darling, no one grows to maturity without changing. You are not the same girl he knew, either. Once this mess is over, you will have time to reacquaint yourselves with one another."

"But that's just it, Papa. I don't want to get to know this Robert."

"Abigail, you are not a child. You not only made a commitment to marry Robert, but you also promised to support him through this ordeal. You cannot abandon him now."

"I will not cry off until the investigation is closed, but Papa, do you realize that he has only called on me once since our betrothal ball? And that he has been distant and, truthfully, unpleasant when I have seen him. I'm not sure he cares for me at all anymore, if he ever did, and—

He smacked his hand on the desk and she jumped. "I don't want to hear any more of this nonsense from you. I must insure your safety and I don't have time to coddle you or deal with your missish concerns. You are a lady and you will start acting like one."

She leapt out of her chair and ran for the door. "Yes, Papa," she whispered as she escaped the study. As she slowly walked to her bedchamber, she realized Papa was correct. After stating publicly that she supported Robert, society would see him as the injured party when she cried off. Her choice was to marry Robert or live her life alone with no hope of having a family of her own.

Still, she would not marry him. If she ended the engagement, there was at least a chance that she might get her fairy tale ending.

Chapter Eleven

Edmund collected Abigail and handed her into the carriage, where Georgiana and Henrietta waited. Her color was high, but he couldn't be sure it had anything to do with him. In any case, his plan to distract her from her situation by inviting her to help him choose a present for his mother seemed to be working. "It is such a fine day it is a shame to take the carriage, but my sisters have convinced me that with three ladies in our party, we shall need the carriage to transport all of our purchases. They insisted on bringing two footmen as well."

He winked at her, then immediately regretted it lest she take offense. He hoped she would enjoy her day of shopping and forget about the stress of the past few weeks, if only for the afternoon. He found himself wishing he had arranged to have Georgiana and Henrietta sit together so he could have Abigail close beside him.

The short ride to Cavendish Square took no time at all.

Edmund helped the ladies exit the carriage and they entered a dress shop where Abigail thought they might have a fichu made for his mother. Discomfort overtook him the moment he entered. Though it was quite fancy for a shop, the air was close and he appeared to be the only male in the building. There were far too many *things* crammed into the space.

Abigail led them up to the counter and inspected several lengths of silk. "What colors does Lady Longcroft favor?"

Edmund frowned. "She only recently switched from black to grey, so it is difficult to say."

"She has also been wearing lavender recently," Henrietta said.

"Lavender? Like the flower? Isn't that just purple?" Women had so confounded many names for colors.

Abigail raised a brow at him. "Lavender is used for half-mourning and is generally much lighter than purple, which is seldom worn by ladies unless they are attempting to attract attention to themselves."

"Aren't women always attempting to attract attention to themselves?"

"Of course not," Georgiana said. "Henrietta tries never to draw attention to herself, and Abigail could certainly do with less attention right now."

Suitably chastised, he said, "Of course. My apologies."

"To get back to the matter at hand, Mama used to enjoy wearing shades of green and gold before Papa died," Henrietta said.

"Let us hope we can convince her to go back to wearing those colors, then, in which case we shall need to choose a fabric that will coordinate with many colors." Abigail turned to him and stared into his eyes, sending his heart pounding.

"Are her eyes the same shade of brown as yours?

He nodded, unable to look away from her intense scrutiny.

"Then gold, or perhaps bronze would suit her well. It shall be up to you and your sisters to convince her that it is time for her to shed her mourning and wear color again."

He must have looked terrified by the prospect because Abigail nearly choked attempting to hold back her laughter.

"What type of fabrics does she favor?"

He shrugged. "The types of fabrics ladies use for gowns, I guess." He pulled at his cravat and shot a panicked look at his sisters. "Henrietta? Georgiana?"

Henrietta spoke first, having spent the most time with their mother at social events. "She used to favor silk, though she may prefer something simpler now that she's a widow."

Abigail's eyes narrowed in consideration. "Still, if she prefers lighter fabrics, she may find she is cold at some of the functions. Perhaps a shawl would be better than a fichu, and easier to remove when the ballroom becomes hot, as it always does."

Edmund nodded. "Yes, that sounds like a practical idea." He understood practical a lot better than he understood fashionable.

She cast him a sideways glance. "No lady ever wants to hear that a gift was chosen for her for practical reasons."

His comfort was short lived. "So ladies prefer impractical gifts?"

Abigail grinned. "Not necessarily, but we don't want to be told that you chose a gift because it was practical. Do you see the difference?"

"Not in the least."

Georgiana exchanged a glance with Abigail and shrugged as if saying, he's all yours.

Abigail returned her gaze to him. "You're supposed to choose a gift because it's pretty or because it made you think of the lady you are purchasing it for. If it's practical that's fine, but for heaven's sake, don't point it out to her."

Edmund momentarily closed his eyes and took a deep breath, recalling the relaxation techniques his fencing master had taught him. "Now I remember why I hate shopping."

Abigail patted his arm in a disappointingly motherly fashion and waved to one of the shop assistants. "We are looking for a special fabric to have a shawl made for the Marchioness of Longcroft."

"Yes, my lady." The girl disappeared through a door and an older woman came out almost immediately.

Abigail conducted the formal introductions to the modiste, which he hoped meant that they could move on with purchasing the shawl before it was time for him to celebrate another birthday. As it turned out, he needn't have worried. He stood back as the four women discussed options.

He studied Abigail's expressions as she shook her head at one fabric and delighted in another. Her features were symmetrical and delicately shaped. He didn't understand how Hinsdale could have thought he needed a mistress when he had her.

They finally settled on a fabric, a strange cream color shot through with gold, silver, and bronze threads. Abigail had been delighted with it as it apparently would match nearly any color gown.

"Would it be possible for you to make matching ribbons? It would be lovely to be able to trim a hat for her to match the shawl."

"That's a grand idea, Abigail." Georgiana leaned closer as the modiste explained their options.

Abigail was certainly in her element here. The modiste excused herself to take care of a few details, and Georgiana retreated to the other side of the room. Abigail turned to him, her face slightly flushed and so happy he had to squash the urge to kiss her. Where had that impulse come from?

She favored him with a mischievous smile. "I've decided on the perfect finishing touch to your gift."

He raised his brows. "Oh you have, have you? The shawl and ribbons aren't enough?"

"The finishing touch would be a new piece of jewelry. Perhaps a comb or pin to hold the shawl. Some other piece that will pull together the gold, silver, and copper elements."

He turned to his sister. "What do you think, Hen?"

"It's an excellent idea. She hasn't had a new piece of jewelry since…well, it's been a long time."

Since their father had died was the thought she failed to voice.

"We'll need to head over to Rundell and Bridge then." He spotted Georgiana coming toward them carrying several parcels. "And what have you been up to while we've been deliberating over presents for our mother?"

"Tish, tosh. We all know Abigail has been doing all the work." Georgiana glanced at her parcels. "I have been making a few purchases, but I shan't go into detail unless you insist since I know you prefer that I not speak about undergarments."

"Heavens, no. Don't you dare." He shot Abigail a long suffering expression and deliberately loosened his cravat.

"Have you finished ordering the shawl?"

She nodded.

"Then I shall go confirm the delivery and then I think we should take a respite from shopping and go to Gunter's for an ice. It's nearly criminal to waste this gorgeous day inside."

Abigail and Henrietta nodded their agreement and went back to discussing the design of a comb. Catching something about raised flowers crafted in various metals, he rushed to escape hearing distance of their conversation and bumped into someone.

Turning to apologize, he discovered it was only Georgiana. "Don't you see enough of me at home? Is it necessary to stay so close here?"

"You know perfectly well we see very little of you at home as you are always tucked away in your study." She turned to meet his eyes. "I wanted to thank you for giving Abigail an occupation. She is much troubled by her situation and needed the distraction."

His stomach tightened. It was the least he could do for her. "It was my pleasure, and I am the one benefitting from her expertise. I daresay mother will be delighted with her gifts."

As he turned away, she said, "And you seem to be benefitting from her attention as well." Unsure how to respond to that, he decided to pretend not to have heard her.

He settled everything with the shop's proprietor and headed back to herd the ladies to the carriage.

He placed a hand on Georgiana's back and guided her toward the door. "Come along now. It's high time for some refreshment. I think I deserve a reward after spending this much time in a dressmaker's shop."

"I fail to see why you find shopping so torturous, but I won't object since I want an ice," said Georgiana as he handed her into the carriage.

Abigail smiled at him. "My father abhors shopping. There must be something built into the male mind that prevents them from enjoying it."

"Perhaps it's something to do with the way it lowers the balance of our accounts."

The ladies exchanged a look but did not retort.

"Let's move on to more important matters," said Henrietta. "What flavor ice does everyone want?"

"Maple," Abigail said immediately.

"Are you sure about that? Perhaps you'd like to think about it a bit more," Edmund teased.

"No, I'm quite certain."

"Georgiana?" he prompted.

"I can't decide between lemon and pineapple."

"Shall I surprise you?" Edmund asked.

"No. I'll go with the lemon."

"I think I shall copy Abigail and try the maple. It must be good if you're that certain," Henrietta said.

"Oh, yes. You won't regret your choice." Abigail set her intense gaze on him, sending a shiver of awareness through him. "What about you?"

"I believe I will stick to the pistachio. Though I've heard the orange is excellent as well." Abigail narrowed her eyes.

"Is something amiss?" he asked.

She shook her head. "No, it's just that I imagined you would enjoy a blander flavor."

He put his hand over his heart. "Why, Lady Abigail. I am

wounded to the core. How can you think me boring?"

"Oh please," Georgiana interjected. "This coming from the man who does not believe in anything that cannot be proven with a mathematical formula."

"You don't believe in anything that can't be proved?" Abigail asked.

"Not that I can think of."

"So you don't believe in love?"

"Not in the sense of falling in love with someone."

Abigail looked stricken. "How can you not believe in love?"

"Love cannot be measured, therefore it does not exist in the romantic manner that you ladies insist upon. Love is expected among family members, of course, but there is certainly no such thing as true love or people who are meant to be together."

Henrietta looked thoughtful. "I don't disagree with him," she said to Abigail. "I'm not certain romantic love isn't just a fleeting fancy."

"My goodness. I had no idea I was surrounded by such an uninspired lot." Georgiana patted Abigail's hand. "You cannot measure beauty either, but surely you can agree that some people are more attractive than others."

He crossed his arms. "I disagree. Beauty can be measured."

Georgiana placed her hands on her hips. "How?"

"Well, we would have to devise a method. First we'd have to define the markers of beauty. Perhaps the color and thickness of hair, the width and color of the eyes, the shape of the face, or length of the nose. Symmetry might come into play. We could easily create markers based on the features of those who are generally thought to be beautiful, and rate the beauty of each individual based on those markers."

"As romantic as that sounds, I think I'll pass." Georgiana paused for a moment, then added, "Although, I do think it would be possible to devise a similar method to measure love."

He lowered his brows and gave her his most stern look. "Impossible."

"Surely not." She grinned. "You could tabulate the number of kind gestures, touches, looks, kisses, intimate moments…"

Good lord. Not only was she wrong, but there was no appropriate way to explain to her that kisses and intimate moments did not necessarily indicate love. He would rather spend the day being trampled by horses than attempt it. He shook his head. "Too arbitrary."

"I disagree."

"On this subject, we are to remain divided."

Abigail narrowed her eyes, revealing an adorable line of disbelief across her nose. Wait. Adorable? He was certain he had never in his life used that word before, and it certainly wasn't an appropriate word to use to describe his sister's closest friend, who happened to be engaged to another man, even if he was a boor.

Thankfully, the carriage was slowing. He glanced out the window into Berkeley Square. He was saved. "Make yourselves comfortable, ladies. I shall go order our ices."

The footmen opened the doors on both sides of the carriage, allowing warm, fresh air to pass through. Edmund stepped down and strode into the shop, where he was immediately acknowledged. After placing their order, he walked back to the carriage, but remained outside, enjoying the unnaturally warm, sunny day. Georgiana and Abigail stepped out to join him.

Before he could come up with suitable topic to discuss, one that had nothing to do with measuring anything, they were approached by a young man of about fourteen or fifteen, he would guess. His clothes were clean and proper, but not expensive. He didn't appear to be dangerous, but nonetheless, Edmund stepped in front of Abigail and Georgiana.

The boy's eyes were trained on Abigail. "My lady, I am John Davies. Sarah Davies was my sister."

Abigail stepped around him to speak with the boy.

Edmund reached to hold her back, then remembered that he ought not to be touching her.

"Hello, John. Is there some way I can be of service to you?"

"My lady, my mother asked me to speak with you, to beg you to call off your marriage to Lord Hinsdale."

Abigail frowned. "And why does she think I should do that?"

"Because he murdered my sister and you are in danger."

Edmund took a step toward Abigail, ready to intervene if necessary.

"The note a little boy gave to me. Was that from your mother?"

The boy shifted his eyes away from her. "You can come out now, Peter."

A much younger boy emerged from behind some bushes. Edmund kept his voice low, hoping not to scare the boys off. "So there was no man in a uniform that asked you to deliver the note to Lady Abigail."

The boy shook his head. "No, my lord. My mother

thought Lady Abigail would be more likely to heed the warning if she thought it came from someone of authority."

"I thank you and your mother for the warning," Abigail said, "but I'm not convinced that Lord Hinsdale is responsible for the death of your sister."

"Oh, but he must be. He promised to marry Sarah, and when he reneged on his promise and she tried to leave, he killed her."

Edmund took a step closer to the boy. "Do you have any proof of his guilt?" The older boy gazed at him with wide, assessing eyes, no doubt wondering if he could be trusted.

The younger boy held onto Abigail's skirts, and she placed her hand atop his head in an unconscious gesture of tenderness. "Does your family live nearby?"

"Just on the edge of Cheapside, my lady. We live above my father's bookshop."

The younger boy slid his hand into Abigail's and she grasped it without hesitation. "Do you think it would be possible for us to meet with your family?"

He kicked at a tuft of grass. "I don't know."

Edmund reached into his pocket for his card and held it out to the boy. "Please tell your parents that Lady Abigail has requested to meet with them. You can send me a note with a convenient time."

He took the card and read it, then placed it in his coat pocket. The boys were clean and well fed, and the older one could read. They were clearly a family of some means and likely had thought serving as a lady's maid was their daughter's chance for a better life. It must have been an unbearable loss for their family.

"I'll speak with them, my lord." The boy waved to his

younger brother, who detached himself from Abigail and followed him. Abigail wiped away a tear and Edmund wanted to pull her into his arms and comfort her.

Georgiana put her arm around Abigail's shoulders. "Abigail, none of this is your fault."

"I know, but I can't help but thinking that none of this would have happened if I hadn't accepted Robert's proposal."

Georgiana shook her head. "If you hadn't, someone else would have."

"I suppose you are correct."

Two waiters approached with their ices, putting an end to the conversation. Edmund handed the ladies back into the carriage and instructed the waiters as to where to deliver the ices.

"Oh, my. This is divine." Abigail closed her eyes, savoring the flavor. Her tongue darted out to catch a stray bit of ice on her lip and Edmund's stomach tightened. He took a bite of his own to distract himself from the idea of licking the ice from her lip himself.

She was correct. He let the ice melt on his tongue, releasing the nutty pistachio flavor that contrasted perfectly with the sweetness of the sugar.

They ate mostly in silence, enjoying the flavorful ice and the warm, sunny day. Yet he sensed none of them would rest comfortably until they heard back from the girl's family.

Chapter Twelve

Abigail held her breath as she walked into yet another ball with a pretend smile forcing her lips to comply. Lord and Lady Nightinger were close friends of her parents, so declining the invitation was out of the question. The only saving grace was that Georgiana and Edmund were also attending, though she had not spotted them yet.

Elinor Price stood alone near the entrance to the card room and Abigail made her way over to her.

"Good evening, Miss Price."

She turned toward Abigail and smiled. "Lady Abigail, how delightful to see you."

"Has my late arrival caused me to miss anything interesting?"

"I'm afraid not. No matter how hard I try, I cannot convince Mama that it is not necessary for us to be the first to arrive at every social function. I believe Lord Hinsdale is in the card room."

Abigail frowned. She was happy to delay their customary

awkward dance until later on. A footman approached and she snagged two glasses of champagne from the tray and handed one to Elinor. "This is so we can start the night on a good note. No more boring conversations and staid dances for us. From now on we will strive to enjoy ourselves."

They clinked their glasses together and Abigail tilted her head back and downed her entire glass. Elinor stared at her with eyes as wide as a startled doe.

Lord Oakley pulled a glass from the tray and paused beside them. He bumped his glass against Abigail's now empty flute. "Ladies, I hope you will both save a dance for me this evening."

"Of course, my lord," they said in unison. He sauntered off as quickly as he had appeared.

Abigail grabbed another glass from the tray of a passing footman, but this one was only lemonade. Though she intended to enjoy herself, she had to mind her behavior. "What do you think of Lady Gressler's gown?"

"Urhm...the copper-ish color is unique."

"Yes, I suppose it is if you are a fan of tarnished silver."

Elinor choked on a sip of champagne and Abigail patted her back.

"What on earth has gotten into you tonight?"

"I'm tired of standing around quietly, waiting on someone else to determine when I can begin to carry on with the rest of my life. I am taking matters into my own hands. I will no longer mope about, but instead will make the decision to enjoy myself."

"I believe that is an excellent plan."

"I'm glad you agree with me." Abigail turned toward the dance floor. "So what do you think of the fit of Lady Gressler's gown?"

Elinor glanced around as if checking to make sure no one else could hear their conversation. "I suppose if I were her, I should like for the bodice to be a bit tighter. And instead of staying with copper tones for everything, I might consider adding a gold sash or some other color to break up the monochromatic scheme."

"I'm pleased to discover that we think alike."

"That is a disturbing discovery, to be sure."

Abigail stiffened at the sound of Edmund's voice, not daring to turn and meet his eyes.

"Good evening, Lady Abigail, Miss Price." He winked at Elinor. "Do not let her get you caught up in her design schemes. She has an opinion about everything and isn't afraid to share it."

Elinor shot Abigail a sideways look. "I shall be on my guard."

"Lady Abigail, would you care to dance?"

"Of course, my lord."

Elinor reached over and plucked the glass from her hand and she shot her a grateful smile.

As they waited for the music to start, Edmund studied her face, but his expression gave away nothing about his thoughts. She breathed in the heady combination of starched shirt and sandalwood and thought she might be able to forget all of her troubles if she could just stay in his arms. He twirled her into the waltz as the music started, and she focused on the warmth of his hand against her back and the gentle comfort that enveloped her within his arms.

He looked down and met her eyes. "You are beautiful tonight."

A jolt went through her at his words, but she tried to

make light of it. "You are quite handsome yourself." Her voice came out in a sultry whisper that did nothing to douse the fire kindling between them. Or perhaps it was just her. He was likely simply being nice. She shook her head and searched for a benign subject to discuss. "Have you seen Lady Needler this evening?"

"No, I'm afraid not. Should I be concerned?"

"Oh, I haven't seen her yet either. That's why I asked. I'm not sure I'm up to reimagining her gown tonight."

"How is Hinsdale holding up?"

Abigail sighed. "I'm afraid I haven't seen him, either."

"I saw him in the card room not long ago."

"Oh." She was more than a bit dismayed to be reminded that though she had attended the ball solely to support him, he still hadn't bothered to seek her out. Was it too much to ask to have the man she was expected to marry to at least attempt to spend time with her instead of hiding in the card room?

He led her to the right to avoid another couple. "Oh, I meant to tell you. The shawl has already arrived and both Georgiana and Henrietta have pronounced it gorgeous and wish to have one made for themselves."

She smiled. "They shall have to create their own designs, then. Has the comb arrived yet?"

"No, but I expected it to take longer than the shawl since it involves delicate metalwork. The jeweler assured me it would be finished on time."

"I hope your mother likes her gifts."

"How could she not?"

"I expect she would appreciate anything you took the time to have made especially for her."

Edmund continued to study her. Abigail's earlier determination to enjoy herself and forget about her worries had fizzled in the reflection of Robert's disinterest. Dancing with Edmund would likely be the only enjoyable portion of an evening that would go on for what seemed an eternity.

"Abigail? You seem worlds away."

"Oh, dear. I've forced you to perform calculations, haven't I?"

"Of course not. Even if you aren't speaking to me, I find myself sufficiently entertained by your presence."

Her heart bumped against her ribs like a moth trapped against a windowpane. "Is that a good thing or a bad thing?"

"Anything having to do with you is always a good thing."

The music stopped playing and he led her back to where he had found her with Elinor. Robert and Georgiana were there as well, and none of them wore a happy expression.

Edmund squeezed her hand briefly before letting go.

"Robert. I hadn't realized you were here." It wasn't strictly true since Elinor had told her of his presence, but he had no way of knowing that.

"Of course you didn't. Surely my betrothed," Robert ground out, "would have chosen to waltz with me had she known I was available."

He snatched her hand and pulled her toward the couples gathering for the next dance. Looking over her shoulder, she caught Georgiana and Edmund exchanging a glance. They took their place in line for a scotch reel, and Edmund and Elinor soon joined them.

"How dare you waltz with him after this afternoon's scandal sheet." Robert shoved the words out through clenched teeth, his lips the only part of his face that moved.

Her stomach jumped, but she refused to allow him to upset her. "I no longer read the scandal sheets. I grew tired of reading about my betrothed in them."

"I remember the words exactly. They are difficult to forget. *Lady A and Lord H are no longer appearing together in public as frequently as they used to. Perhaps Lady A is beginning to believe the stories of his guilt. Could the end be near?*" He glared down at her. "The problem is not that we are together with less frequency, but that you are spending more and more time with Longcroft. How do you defend yourself?"

How dare he? When he had...she took three slow, measured breaths to calm herself before responding. "I don't need to defend myself. I have done nothing wrong. Lord Longcroft frequently escorts Lady Georgiana and I. You know that. It is not a new phenomenon."

"You are making a fool of me."

Abigail barely refrained from telling him he was doing that on his own. Instead, she said, "My behavior has not changed. The gossips are simply looking for anything that will keep society embroiled in your affairs. Perhaps we would be better served by acting graciously toward one another rather than arguing in a crowded ballroom about things we cannot control."

His eyes simmered with anger, but he stopped his inquisition, and in fact, stopped speaking with her at all, which suited her very well.

Abigail shot Elinor a smile. If nothing else, it gave her an excuse to look away from Robert's seething anger. The music served as a stay of execution and Abigail thanked the stars it was a scotch reel and not the waltz where they would have been trapped together.

The lilt of Elinor's laughter floated to her, an example of how her evening should have been unfolding. She focused on the dancers around them and made it through to the end. Robert took her back to where Georgiana and Abigail's mother were standing, arriving just ahead of Elinor and Edmund.

Obviously sensing Robert's sour mood, her mother attempted to take charge of the situation. "Lord Hinsdale, are you acquainted with Miss Price? I believe she is available for the next dance."

"Yes, of course. Good evening, Miss Price." He glanced at Abigail and then back to Elinor. "I'm afraid I am already engaged." He turned and left without another word and disappeared into the card room.

Abigail wished she could disappear as well. How dare he refuse to dance with Elinor? Perhaps there had been a new development with the case that had caused him more anxiety, but still, that was no excuse for his pigheaded behavior.

"Miss Price, Lady Abigail, I find myself a trifle overheated after that reel. Would you care to explore the terrace? I hear Lady Nightinger has some extraordinary plants on display."

Thank goodness for Edmund's quick thinking. Elinor nodded, her eyes glistening with unshed tears. Abigail clasped her arm and marched onto the terrace with her.

"Ah, there it is, Lady Nightinger's famous purple rose." Edmund pointed to a large pot sheltered against the house in a corner of the terrace.

Abigail pulled Elinor toward the flowers, appreciating Edmund's efforts to distract her from Robert's outrageous behavior. The rose petals were soft and smooth. She gently cupped a flower in her palm and inhaled the fragrance. "It is a lovely color. Do you know how she came to have it?"

Edmund touched one of the petals. "I'm not certain, but I have heard that her gardener in Sussex came across a purple bud unexpectedly in her greenhouse."

Elinor's blank stare vanished as she took interest in the conversation. She came forward and smelled the flower just as Abigail had done. "But how could a purple flower just appear in her greenhouse?"

"Though all of the details have yet to be discovered, a German botanist named Rudolf Camerarius isolated the parts of a flower that work together to produce seeds." He moved forward between the two ladies.

"See here?" He pointed to the center of the flower. "This is the stamen, the male organ of the flower, and this the pistil, the female organ. Both are required to produce seeds."

Abigail raised a brow at Elinor, and they both leaned closer.

"See this yellow, powdery substance? That is pollen produced by the male organ, which plays a role in making seeds. Of course, unlike animals, plants cannot move about in order to reproduce, so the mystery is how a single type of rose could produce a different color of flower. Likely there were other types of roses in the greenhouse that somehow combined to create the purple roses."

Elinor bit her lip and widened her eyes at Abigail, who looked away to prevent a giggle from escaping. Ever the academic, poor Edmund didn't seem to realize his information was a bit saucy for two unmarried females, and yet, she greatly appreciated his attempts to distract Elinor. If only Robert possessed the same considerate nature.

"Not all flowers have both a pistil and stamen, however."
He glanced around the terrace and strode to another pot of
flowers. "See these lilies? They can have either a pistil or a
stamen, but never both in the same flower."

Abigail leaned over to look into the lily, heat creeping
up her neck into her face. Careful to avoid eye contact
with Elinor lest they burst out laughing, she focused on the
structure of the flower. "It is different. How remarkable. I
must confess I've never considered how flowers…ehrm…
duplicate."

"I can't say that I have either, but it's quite a fascinating
subject," Elinor added. "Especially the ability to create
different colors and varieties."

Abigail exchanged another glance with Elinor. "I suppose
we should be heading back to the ballroom before we are
missed. Thank you for escorting us, Lord Longcroft. I believe
fresh air was just what we needed to revive ourselves."

• • •

Edmund held out his arm to Abigail on one side and Elinor
on the other. He noted that Abigail's ears were startlingly
red. She exchanged a glance with Miss Price, and both bit
back smiles. A quick giggle erupted, but he wasn't sure which
lady it came from.

Good lord. Had he really just given two innocent ladies
a detailed explanation of plant copulation? He would have
loosened his cravat had he a free hand.

Although, it had certainly been effective as a distraction.

He led them back to the ballroom and escaped into the
card room as quickly as possible. Populated with elderly

matrons and only the most dedicated of gamblers, it was a place he normally avoided. At least there were no young girls present whose innocence he could compromise.

He discovered Hinsdale once again playing hazard. Taking a seat at an open spot at one of the whist tables, he settled in to observe his behavior.

"Lord Longcroft, would you care to deal?" asked his partner, the Dowager Countess of Kenner.

"It would be my pleasure, Lady Kenner." He winked at her and dealt the cards while keeping one eye on Hinsdale. He had just bet ten pounds on a single roll of the dice. His behavior was spiraling out of control and Lord Wrexham needed to rein him in before it was too late.

Edmund turned his attention to the game and sped through a full rubber of whist. He collected his winnings and stood. "Lady Kenner, it has been a pleasure, but I'm afraid I must return to the ballroom." He kissed her cheek and bit back a smile when she blushed.

She placed her hand on his sleeve. "Are you certain you must leave? We make a good team."

"Yes, we do, but if too many of the gentlemen spend the evening in the card room, the young ladies will have no one to dance with." He squeezed her hand and headed for the door.

"All right, off with you then. I shall find another partner, though he's not likely to be as handsome as you," she called after him.

The moment he entered the ballroom, he spotted Georgiana and Abigail deep in conversation. Georgiana looked up as his shadow fell across them. "We were beginning to despair of you and feared we might be stranded here all night."

He raised his brows.

"Lady Jaffrey took ill while Abigail was in the middle of a set. Since Lord Jaffrey didn't wish to interrupt, I assured him that you would be pleased to see her home."

He nodded.

"You don't mind, do you? It isn't too far out of the way."

"Of course not, though it would be nice to be consulted every once in a while before decisions are made." He winked at Abigail. "Having six busybody sisters can wear a man down, make him feel like he's not the master of his own home."

Georgiana snorted and Abigail slapped a hand over her mouth in an effort to contain her giggle. He was glad to see her in better spirits after the way her idiotic future husband had treated her earlier. As if the thought had conjured him, Hinsdale crossed the ballroom and headed for the front door without acknowledging Abigail.

Remembering his recent conversation with Lord Wrexham, a sudden idea struck him. "Are you ladies up for some sleuthing tonight?"

"We are always up for some sleuthing, aren't we, Abigail?"

Abigail nodded, her determined gaze never leaving Edmund, spurring him to help her learn once and for all whether Hinsdale was guilty of something other than disgraceful behavior. "Then let us make haste. I shall explain in the carriage."

Edmund waited impatiently for the carriage to be brought around, with Georgiana and Abigail shooting him curious glances every few seconds.

It wouldn't do to follow Hinsdale too closely as Edmund's carriage was easily recognizable, but since he had only a rough idea of where the man lived, they needed to keep him in sight. Finally the carriage arrived and he all but tossed the ladies in. Dashing up to the box, he instructed his coachman. "Follow the carriage that just left, but don't get close enough to be recognized."

He leapt in and rapped on the ceiling to indicate they should leave.

"What in the world are you about?" Georgiana asked.

"I spoke with Lord Wrexham recently and he mentioned that Hinsdale has moved into bachelor's quarters. I thought we could follow him."

Georgiana narrowed her eyes. "Toward what end? Do you expect to see him hiding a body?"

Abigail's face immediately drained of color.

"Georgiana, mind your tongue."

She recoiled at his rebuke and turned to Abigail. "I'm sorry, dearest, sometimes my mouth works faster than my brain, as you well know."

"Pay me no heed." Abigail patted Georgiana's hand. "He is accused of murder, after all. Finding him standing over a body would at least put an end to this endless speculation."

Georgiana giggled, and Abigail followed suit. Edmund shook his head. More often than not, women were an enigma.

Abigail struggled to force words out through her giggles. "Now I'm…picturing him…trying to drag a body through…"

She couldn't even finish her sentence she was laughing so hard, and Georgiana was no better.

Thankfully the carriage slowed to a stop and saved him the need to try to make sense of their conversation. He opened the door and stuck his head out.

The coachman said, "My lord, he entered a house down the street. Michael can point it out to you if you like."

"Thank you, Clarence." He turned back to the ladies. The

proper thing would be to leave them in the carriage while he investigated, but even though he trusted his coachman to keep them safe, he didn't trust the women to stay put. No, it would be better to keep them where he could see them.

He waved them forward. "Follow me. Stay low and be quiet."

Michael pointed to Hinsdale's residence. It was a decent sized house that had likely been divided into separate apartments. Edmund led them across the street where they could remain in the shadows and watch the house for any movement.

"What do you expect to happen?" Georgiana whispered.

"I don't know. I hadn't thought any further than confirming his address."

"There he is." Abigail pointed to a third floor window.

Hinsdale stood in front of the window, illuminated from behind by candlelight or a lamp. He seemed to be looking right at them before he turned his back to the window. A set of slim, bare arms slid around him and Abigail sucked in a strangled breath.

Good lord. The grass hadn't even grown over the grave of his previous mistress and he already had another one. At least, Edmund hoped it was a mistress and not a prostitute. Georgiana was already leading Abigail back to the carriage. He watched for a few more minutes, but there was nothing of use to be seen.

He had made a terrible error in judgment. He should never have brought Georgiana and especially Abigail here, but he never dreamed anything like this would happen. Damn Hinsdale for being a reprobate, and damn him for allowing his attraction to Abigail to cloud his judgment and cause her more pain.

Chapter Thirteen

Abigail lay on her bed, studying the pattern on her ceiling created by the sunlight filtering through her curtains. Sadness for what her betrothal to Robert should have been left her head aching. After giving Baxter's head one last stroke, she sat up. When she broke off her engagement, she would have to resign herself to a life alone. She wished there was another option for her, but she knew without doubt that she could not live with herself if she went through with the marriage.

Despite his deplorable conduct, she didn't believe him to be a killer, but she also did not wish to spend the rest of her life subject to the sort of behavior she had witnessed in him over the past weeks. She would be better off living out her life alone, serving as the doting aunt to her brothers' children. In a few years, she might even be able to set up a household of her own. It wasn't how she had envisioned her life, but marriage to Robert came at too high a price. She would find a time to convince Papa of the wisdom of her decision once the murder was solved.

Preferring solitude, she passed the morning in her bedchamber. Though it was Judith's day off, she decided to clean out her wardrobe. She needed something to occupy her mind, which kept conjuring up images of Edmund. Even if there were a possibility that he might return her feelings, it wouldn't be fair to Georgiana or her younger sisters to contaminate their family with the gossip that would surely follow Abigail no matter what she did.

She shook her head and focused on her wardrobe. First she selected three gowns she hadn't worn all season and placed them on the bed, followed by several night rails and two hats she no longer fancied. Judith would take what she wanted and offer the rest to the other maids.

A knock sounded on the door and she opened it to find George. "You've already finished your tutoring for the day?"

He shook his head. "Not quite, but we were working outside and mother sent me to fetch you. Lady Georgiana is here."

She and Baxter followed George downstairs and found Georgiana waiting in the parlor with her maid.

Georgiana turned away from the window and hurried over. "Thank goodness you are at home. Edmund received a note from Sarah's family this morning. They would like us to call on them this afternoon."

"Then we should leave immediately." She turned to rush from the room and nearly smacked into her mother. Studying her startled face, Abigail deduced that she had not overheard their conversation. "Mama, I was just coming to find you. I am going to Longcroft Hall for the afternoon. Georgiana has asked me to help with preparations for

Elizabeth's come out." The latter was true, it just wasn't what they would be doing today. She hated that Robert had put her in a position where she had to lie to her parents, but they would never give her permission to accompany Georgiana and Edmund to visit Sarah's family.

"My goodness. It seems as if you are never at home anymore. When should we expect you back?"

She shrugged. "I have no idea. There is much to be done. Am I needed for anything here?"

"No, I suppose not."

"Then I shall see you when I return." Abigail kissed her cheek.

They wasted no time walking to Longcroft Hall. The carriage awaited them, as did Edmund.

"Were you able to locate Henrietta?" Georgiana asked him.

"She is off on an errand and has sent instructions for us to carry on without her."

Though Henrietta had briefly been married, she now enjoyed a life of freedom. Abigail would one day be able to do the same as a lady who was firmly on the shelf. She would just have to be patient until then.

Edmund held out his hand and she clasped it to climb into the carriage. A wash of excitement shot through her, as it always did at his touch. Once Georgiana was settled, he climbed in and sat on the seat across from them.

"I have instructed the coachman to drop us off and take the carriage to Covent Garden to await our return. There's no reason to arouse suspicion by leaving the carriage on the street in Cheapside."

Abigail remained quiet, wondering how Sarah's family

would feel about her being at their home. Did they blame her for making it impossible for Robert to marry Sarah? Worse, did they blame her for Sarah's death? Perhaps she ought not to have come, though the family had attempted to warn her against Robert. Surely they would not have done that if they thought her at fault. She would discover their opinion of her soon enough. The ride passed quickly and before she could change her mind again, they were in front of the bookshop.

The older boy who had approached them outside Gunter's emerged from the shop and led them behind the building where a staircase led to the family's living quarters. They mounted the stairs and the boy held the door open for them to enter.

Edmund removed his hat and held his hand out to the middle aged couple standing before them. "Mr. and Mrs. Davies, thank you for agreeing to meet with us. As you have probably deduced from my card, I am the Marquess of Longcroft." He pointed to Georgiana. "This is my sister, Lady Georgiana, and this is Lady Abigail, the daughter of Lord Jaffrey."

Mrs. Davies put her hand to her mouth and took a deep, shuddering breath.

Abigail didn't think she could feel any more uncomfortable.

Mr. Davies patted his wife's hand and motioned toward the table. "Please, take a seat."

Their apartment consisted of one large room divided into a kitchen, a study, and a sitting area. Two other rooms, presumably bedrooms, opened off of the main room. Pillows and curtains in bright yellow and blue would have made the room cheerful and welcoming under different circumstances.

They all sat, with Abigail sandwiched between Edmund and Georgiana.

Mrs. Davies brought a tea tray to the table and the older boy set a tray of biscuits next to it.

"Would you care for tea?" she asked.

Edmund shook his head, but Abigail and Georgiana both accepted a cup. Abigail preferred to have something with which to occupy her hands.

"I know how difficult this must be for you, but we do hope to help by determining who is responsible for this horrible crime," Edmund said.

Mrs. Davies met Abigail's eyes. "Do you truly not believe that Lord Hinsdale is guilty?"

Abigail shook her head. "Though the circumstances have forced me to uncover some unpleasant facets of Lord Hinsdale's personality, I do not think him guilty of murder, though he is certainly to blame for exercising poor judgment."

Mrs. Davies bit her lip. "I want you to know that my Sarah would never have taken up with Lord Hinsdale if she hadn't thought he would marry her. She wasn't that sort of girl." She stifled a sob. "He said he would marry her. She never lied."

"Now dearest, there's no need to upset yourself." Her husband patted her arm. "They understand."

Abigail bowed her head, the knot in her stomach proof enough that she didn't doubt Sarah's word.

Mr. Davies folded his hands on the table. "The authorities are either keeping us in the dark as far as the investigation is concerned, or they haven't made any headway."

Edmund nodded. "Both Lord Wrexham and Lord Hinsdale voluntarily submitted to an interview with the magistrate, and they have been interviewing the servants at Wrexham House."

"The only person we have heard from was the coroner." He glanced at his wife before continuing. "But his part in the investigation is over."

"As I'm sure you can understand, until the case is solved we are concerned for the safety of Lady Abigail. Toward that end, we are conducting investigations of our own. Is there anything you can think of that might help us?" Edmund glanced at Abigail as she crossed her arms over her stomach and pressed against it, willing it to settle.

"The coroner told us she was strangled. I can't help but think the murderer might have used one of her ribbons to do it." Mrs. Davies forced the soft words through trembling lips, making them all the more devastating.

"Her ribbons?" Edmund asked.

Mrs. Davies went to the chest of drawers in the kitchen area and began rummaging around. "Sarah loved hair ribbons. Ever since she was a little girl she had a huge collection of them." She pulled a ribbon from one of the drawers and brought it back to the table. "As she got older, she began to embroider them with intricate patterns."

Returning to the table, she stroked her fingers across the surface of the material before handing the ribbon to Abigail.

The needlework was very fine. "This is remarkable work. So much detail." This particular ribbon was covered with flowers embroidered in various shapes, sizes, and colors.

Mrs. Davies wiped a tear from her face and Abigail reached over and took her hand. "The coroner told us that the object used to…to kill Sarah was flat and wide and may have left an odd pattern on her neck, though it was difficult to discern be…because she had been in the water."

Abigail squeezed her hand. "Do you know of anyone she was close to at Wrexham House?"

"Just Lady Jane. Sarah was only three years older than the girl." Overcome with grief, Mrs. Davies sobbed and her husband pulled her into his arms. Knowing her sadness was nothing compared to what Mrs. Davies experienced, Abigail wiped away a tear and concentrated on her breathing.

Edmund reached for her hand under the table in what seemed an unconscious act of comfort. "Did she ever mention any of the male servants? An admirer, perhaps?"

The older boy, who had remained in the shadows of the kitchen while they spoke, approached the table. "She once told me that one of the grooms attempted to corner her in the corridor to the kitchen, and they frequently fought over who would accompany Sarah and Lady Jane when they went out."

Edmund straightened in his chair. "Did she mention any names?"

The boy shrugged. "Not that I can remember. She did say that one of the grooms was reprimanded for behaving inappropriately around her and Lady Jane."

Abigail exchanged a look with Edmund. Reassured by his calm demeanor and reasoned questions, she left the interview to him. "When was that?" he asked the boy.

"Let's see. I remember her bringing Lady Jane to visit the bookshop not long after that." He turned to his father. "Do you remember when that was, Papa?"

"At least six months ago. Lady Jane has patronized the shop several times since then."

"Did she have any valuables to support the theory that

she was robbed by a stranger?" Georgiana asked.

Mr. Davies shook his head. "Not that we know of. But the police said a footpad would attack without knowing whether there was a reward to be had."

Straightening in her seat, Mrs. Davies dried her eyes on her apron. "The police also said that strangulation is an intimate crime. That the perpetrator often knows the victim."

Abigail shared another pointed look with Edmund. They were back to Robert as the prime suspect again.

Mrs. Davies reached for Abigail's hand. "I'm so sorry if the note we sent scared you, but I was concerned about your safety and wanted to frighten you into leaving Lord Hinsdale. Even if he isn't guilty, I hope you'll reconsider your future. I do think there is someone else out there who would be better for you."

Mrs. Davies cast her gaze at Edmund, and Abigail's face heated. Mrs. Davies wasn't suggesting anything she hadn't already though about herself, but that didn't mean Edmund had any interest in her. He was simply helping with the investigation because Georgiana had asked him to and not because he had any regard for her beyond friendship. No sane man would want to become tainted by the scandal surrounding her.

"Sometimes I wonder about that as well," she said to Mrs. Davies.

There didn't seem to be anything more to learn from Sarah's family, so they thanked them and took their leave.

• • •

Most of the ride back to Longcroft passed in silence. The

pain and indecision on Abigail's face was palpable. Edmund wanted to pull her into his arms, to hold and comfort her. But for heaven's sake, she was engaged to marry another man. And a peer at that. He hoped she would cry off because he did not wish to see her trapped in a miserable marriage with Hinsdale, but he certainly would not attempt to influence her decision. This was what happened when one let his emotions rule instead of his head. He simply needed to perform some calculations to get his mind back in order. His conversation with Georgiana about being able to measure love popped into his head. What a ridiculous pursuit that would be. And yet it wouldn't leave his mind.

As they neared Longcroft, he had a sudden idea. "Abigail, if you are not otherwise engaged, would you care to join us for tea? I believe we would do well to discuss our next move and come up with a plan of action."

Georgiana's brows shot up when he called her Abigail, but it seemed ridiculous to be so formal when they had been sleuthing and spying on Hinsdale in the middle of the night together.

After glancing at Georgiana, she said, "I am available and could definitely use some tea."

As they entered the house, Abigail and Georgiana headed for the parlor while Edmund went to his study to fetch the notes he had been keeping on the investigation. He rushed back down the corridor just in time to see Elizabeth and Lady Jane slip into the parlor ahead of him. Jane's presence would make it difficult to hold their discussion. Perhaps they should retreat to his study. He came to a halt in the doorway.

Lady Jane turned to him. "I hope you don't mind the

intrusion, Lord Longcroft, but I hoped to speak to Lady Abigail."

"Not at all," he said, extending his hand toward the settee.

Choosing to sit next to Abigail, she made herself comfortable as everyone waited for her to speak. "I know something that might be of use in the inquest, but no one will listen to me. I tried to tell Papa, but he forbid me to talk to the investigators and threatened to exile me to Wrexham Park."

Abigail smiled at her. "What is it you wish to share?"

"Sarah was very fond of ribbons. She told me she often felt invisible as a maid and took great pride in embroidering her ribbons with intricate patterns and bright colors."

Edmund leaned forward on his seat. "How does this relate to the murder?"

Jane mirrored his movement. "When Sarah left, she took all of her ribbons with her, but I overheard the inspector talking to Papa. He said that there was only a small satchel of clothes with her when she was found. But I know that she had more belongings than that, including all of her ribbons."

As the only man in a household of six women, he was attuned to nuances of inappropriate behavior, but now was not the time to chastise her for eavesdropping.

"Are you certain she took everything with her? Did she say where she was going?" Georgiana asked.

Lady Jane nodded. "She was going back to her family and planned to work in their book shop until she could find another position as a maid."

"Perhaps she left her belongings with the housekeeper, then, and was planning to send her father or brother to fetch them?"

She shook her head. "No. Since I wasn't allowed to

attend the ball, I saw her off myself. All of the servants were busy. She left carrying two large bags along with her satchel, but only her satchel was found."

Abigail turned to him. "That would support the theory that it was the work of a thief."

"Except that one of our footmen has one of her ribbons," Lady Jane said.

They all turned to stare at her.

"Are you certain?" asked Georgiana.

She nodded.

"How can we be sure she did not give it to him?"

"Sarah only had eyes for Robert. Though she liked him, she never would have given one of her ribbons to Thomas. They were too recognizable and would have been viewed as a sign of her favor."

Edmund straightened. "Did you ever witness Thomas bothering Sarah?"

"No, but Sarah frequently went about her chores without me. She mentioned him more than once because he always went out of his way to talk to her."

"And you saw him with one of her ribbons after she died?"

She nodded.

"But you had not seen him with it before she left?"

"No. I'm certain Sarah did not give him a ribbon."

Though it might be a fool's errand, he had to share this information. It was worth looking into, and it wasn't as if they had any other leads to follow.

Edmund stood and walked to Lady Jane. "This might not mean anything, but it could be important. I will go speak with your father. I understand his desire to keep you away from the inquest, but this information could exonerate your brother."

"I must confess that is exactly what I had hoped. He will listen to you."

He turned to Abigail and Lady Jane. "I shall take the carriage to call on Lord Wrexham. May I see you home?"

As he ushered them to the carriage, excitement built within him that this would be the break in the case they had all been waiting for. Whether Hinsdale was found guilty or innocent, Abigail would finally be able to break her engagement and shed the yoke that had prevented her from moving on to a more promising future.

Chapter Fourteen

The next morning, Edmund waited once again for Abigail and Henrietta to arrive so he could explain the results of his meeting with Lord Wrexham. In the meantime, he dabbled with a formula he had created to measure beauty. However, no matter how he tried, he could not devise one formula to measure love. Perhaps the problem was that there were too many variables to fit into one equation. Thankfully, the front door squeaked opened, indicating that at least one of his visitors had arrived, rescuing him from further work on the confounded formula.

Henrietta had brought Abigail in her carriage, so everyone was waiting on him when he entered the parlor.

"How do you ladies feel about a trip to the theater tonight?" he asked.

"Why?" Georgiana asked, clearly skeptical.

Henrietta narrowed her eyes. "Perhaps you should start at the beginning. What happened with the footman?"

"I was unable to confirm Lady Jane's suspicions about the ribbon because the footman named Thomas resigned his position at Wrexham House. However, I have it on good authority that he is now working at Covent Garden."

Georgiana wiggled in her seat. "So he is likely guilty since he quit. He's running away."

"Actually, no. I did speak with Lord Wrexham about Jane's concerns, but the Bow Street runner Wrexham hired interviewed Thomas, along with all of the other servants, the day after the ball. Thomas was present throughout the entire ball, and there are witnesses to confirm his statement."

Abigail sighed. "So he could not have been the murderer."

"Lady Jane did say that he and Sarah were friendly with one another, so he didn't necessarily have a motive for killing her. But, there is still the matter of the ribbon. I propose that we attend the theater tonight and track down Thomas so we can ask him point blank about the ribbon."

When no one responded, Edmund glanced around at the dejected faces of Abigail and his sisters. "Do none of you enjoy the theater? Come now. It has been too long since we've used our box." He walked to the table and picked up *The Morning Post*. "*Zembuca* is showing. The paper states that it 'captured the voluptuous splendor of the East,' producing effects 'little less than magical.'"

"It's not that we don't enjoy the theater," Abigail said, "it's just that I think we were all hoping to hear that the murderer had been found."

Edmund smiled at her earnest expression. She had the right of it. They were all weary of the investigation. "That is understandable, but if the footman does have one of Sarah's ribbons, then he may have valuable information. I think we are very close to solving this mystery."

"All right, Abigail and I will accompany you," Georgiana said. "Hen, are you available?"

"I'm afraid not, as I am to dine with a neighbor. You will update me immediately if you learn anything, won't you?"

"Of course we will." Georgiana patted her leg.

Edmund briefly wondered which neighbor could be more interesting than a murder investigation, but decided it wasn't worth pursuing.

"If you ladies will excuse me, I have some work to finish." Something Abigail had said had gotten him thinking about a love formula and how he might be trying to force together variables that didn't necessarily mesh. With luck, he could solve the formula before they headed to the theater, and he could prove to himself that his interest in Abigail wasn't of a romantic nature, but simply attraction to a like-minded person. Because true romantic love did not exist.

$\cdots$

The Post had the right of it about *Zembuca*. It did not take a genius to determine to whom the author was referring when the evil tyrant was overthrown, and the effects were rather spectacular. And yet, Abigail had difficulty focusing on the show while trying to locate the footman from Wrexham. After leaving Longcroft that afternoon, she had gone to see Jane to get a description and a rough sketch of Thomas. So far, there had been no sign of him.

She sidled closer to Edmund, the one place where she always seemed to feel more at ease. "Shall we request more food or champagne? The evening is winding down, and we still haven't seen Thomas."

He glanced at the other occupants of the box, which included Georgiana and several acquaintances who had come to visit with Edmund when they discovered that he had finally come to the theater. "I suppose so. I would prefer to go in search of him, but I doubt we would be able to gain access to the servants' chambers."

"Yes, I expect you are correct."

Edmund squeezed her hand and exited the box to request more of something edible. By now, the footmen must be wondering if they were secretly keeping an elephant in this box with the amount of food they had gone through. Abigail was so full that she thought they might have to dump the food out somewhere and pour the champagne into the potted plants.

Her hand still tingled where he had touched her. If only she could finally end her betrothal with Robert, she thought perhaps a relationship with Edmund might be possible. Though he was drawn into her life out of obligation to his sisters, she dared to hope that he might return her feelings.

Edmund returned a short time later and moved to speak with one of his roommates from Oxford. Abigail continued to hang back, out of her element among so many people she didn't know well. She admired Georgiana's ability to converse freely with everyone. She never seemed to feel awkward or run out of things to discuss as Abigail did. Other than her father, Edmund was the only man she truly felt comfortable conversing with.

A footman she hadn't seen yet entered the box carrying yet another tray of *hors d'oeuvre*. She quickly glanced at Jane's sketch. Tall, dark hair, horizontal scar on his chin. She waved at Edmund, who was still engaged in conversation at the front of the box. His eyes flicked to her briefly and she hoped he saw the footman and understood. Not wanting to lose track of him, she followed the footman into the corridor when he left.

"What are you doing?" Edmund asked from close behind her.

"Following him. Based on Jane's description, I think he is Thomas."

"You should have waited for me."

"There was no time. I didn't want him to get away."

Edmund released a long-suffering sigh. "Are you certain it's him?"

"He matches Jane's description, including the scar on his chin."

Edmund marched past her and shoved her behind him. "Excuse me. May I have a word?" he called down the corridor.

The footman stopped and turned to meet his eyes.

"Are you by any chance a former employee of Lord Wrexham?"

"Yes, my lord. I worked as a footman at Wrexham House until recently. How may I help you?"

"I am Lord Longcroft, and this is Lady Abigail Hurst, who as you may know, is betrothed to Lord Hinsdale."

"Yes, my lord. I am Thomas Dunfrey." He bowed.

Thomas not only didn't attempt to leave, but also didn't show any sign of being nervous or uncomfortable. Abigail did not think he was guilty of anything. Robert showed more agitation daily than he exhibited.

"Thomas, I would like to ask you a few questions about Sarah Davies," Edmund said.

He glanced at Abigail before responding. "I will speak

with you, my lord, but could we move to a more private location? I don't wish to risk my position here. There is an empty chamber just down the way."

"Yes, of course." Edmund took Abigail's arm and they followed him.

After closing the curtain, he turned to them. "I didn't kill Sarah. I loved her. I proposed to her several times. Even after she took up with Lord Hinsdale, begging your pardon, my lady, I pleaded with her to marry me and leave Wrexham House, but she refused. I knew the coxcomb…"—he took a deep breath and continued—"she thought Lord Hinsdale would marry her, but I knew he wouldn't."

"Thomas, do you have any of Sarah's hair ribbons? The ones that she embroidered herself?"

"I do, my lord."

"Did Sarah give them to you?"

"No, my lord. I have only one." He reached inside his coat and withdrew the ribbon. It was light blue in color and embroidered with tiny flowers. "Lady Jane's new maid, Mary, gave it to me. Said she found them in the cabinet in her chamber when she moved in."

Abigail took a step toward Thomas. "Do you think Lord Hinsdale killed Sarah?"

"No, my lady. Begging your pardon once again, but he doesn't seem the type to do something like that on his own, and it would be too much of a risk to hire someone else to do it." Thomas glanced toward the floor. "I don't think he cared enough about her to bother."

"Do you have any idea who might have done it?"

"No, my lord. I figured she was set upon by thieves when she left." He turned away and wiped at his eyes before continuing. "I told her I would take her home after the ball, but she wouldn't wait. I had already decided to leave Wrexham House, but I needed the reference to get the position here. I couldn't leave during the ball."

Abigail wished futilely that Sarah had accepted Thomas's offer.

Edmund reached out and shook his hand. "Thank you for speaking with us, Thomas. You've been very helpful."

Abigail gave him her hand. "Thank you, Thomas. I wish you well."

Thomas left, and Edmund turned to her. "We must determine whether Jane is correct about Sarah taking the ribbons with her when she left. If she did take them, we need to focus on Jane's new maid."

Abigail thought for a moment. "I have several younger brothers. When one does something wrong, it's usually not difficult to determine who is guilty because they squirm around and avoid making eye contact. I think we need to go to Wrexham House and confront the maid and see how she reacts."

Edmund placed his hands on her shoulders and turned her toward him. "Correction. *I* need to go to Wrexham House and confront the maid. You are not to be involved in this."

She narrowed her eyes. "I'm already involved. Remember, I'm the reason you are involved, and I'm sorry to have dragged you into all of this, but I'm very grateful for your assistance and support."

He took a step closer and pushed a stray lock of hair behind her ear, then kept his palm resting against the back of her head. He leaned toward her and slowly pulled her toward him. Her pulse thrummed through her. His warmth enveloped her along with his heady scent of citrus and sandalwood.

"Edmund?" Georgiana's stage whisper floated in from the corridor and they jumped apart. He cleared the thickness from his throat before responding.

"Georgiana? You better have a very good excuse for wandering about the theater unchaperoned."

She stalked into the box. "You left without me. One moment you two were there, and the next I was alone with your university chums. How is that any worse than wandering the corridors alone?"

"My apologies for not alerting you, but we needed to act quickly to follow Thomas."

"You found him?"

"Yes, and he is most certainly not guilty of killing Sarah." Edmund ran his hands through his hair. "Did you simply sneak out of the box?"

Georgiana frowned at her brother. "Of course not. I told them Abigail hadn't been feeling well earlier and I feared she might have become ill."

"Very well, I will go back to the box and apologize, and then I'm going to take you two home so I can go to Wrexham immediately."

"What? Why?"

"Abigail will explain."

• • •

Abigail and Georgiana had managed to badger Edmund into taking them with him to Wrexham House, but he steadfastly refused to allow them to the leave the carriage. Georgiana had dozed off, but Abigail was too nervous and excited to sleep. Edmund had been about to kiss her when Georgiana interrupted. This could finally be the end of the investigation, or just another dead end, but either way, there was a chance that Edmund might return her feelings.

Finally, footsteps approached and the carriage shifted as someone climbed down off the box. The door opened and Edmund climbed in, but his expression revealed nothing.

Georgiana didn't stir. Edmund placed his finger to his lips and beckoned Abigail to move next to him.

"It is over. Luck was on our side tonight and the Bow Street runner happened to be here."

"And?" Abigail prompted when he failed to continue.

"Jane was right. Sarah had taken all of her belongings with her. And you were also correct about Mary. When questioned, she admitted that she had convinced the groom Jane mentioned to follow Sarah when she left and steal anything of value she had. She claims not to have asked him to kill Sarah, but that remains to be determined. The magistrate has been summoned to take them both away."

Abigail leaned back against the seat, not sure what to think or do.

Edmund moved closer and ran the pad of his finger over her lips, sending tingles shooting across them. She kissed his finger, then leaned toward him —

"What did I miss?" Georgiana straightened on the seat and rubbed her eyes, and though Abigail loved her dearly, she briefly contemplated shoving Georgiana from the carriage. Instead, she sat back and waited for Edmund to begin his story again.

Chapter Fifteen

Abigail had been much too excited to sleep when she returned home last night. Edmund had nearly kissed her. Twice. A part of her wanted to immediately break off her engagement to Robert and rush into Edmund's arms. He was kind and honorable and made her feel safe. But, even if he felt the same way about her that she did about him, was it fair to allow her scandal to taint his family, and possibly affect her dearest friend's chances on the marriage mart?

No matter, even if it meant spending her life alone, she would end her betrothal to Robert, with or without her father's permission. She attempted to compose herself before seeking him out. She smoothed her hair and pinched her cheeks to dispel the pallor of her skin. As was his habit at this time of the morning, Papa was in his study.

"Papa, I have the most extraordinary news. The killer of Lady Jane's maid has been found. Robert is exonerated."

Silence reigned for several seconds as he studied her

face. "Where did you hear this?"

"From Georgiana. Lord Longcroft's butler is the cousin of a footman at Wrexham House." Though that was not precisely how she found out, it was not an untruth. "I expect the news will be spread across all of London within the hour."

"I see. I cannot deny that this is excellent news, but you don't appear to be relieved."

No, unless someone had the power to turn back the clocks to prevent Sarah's murder, there was nothing about the situation that could give her relief. "I am quite pleased that Robert is truly not guilty, but Papa, I do not think I can go through with our marriage." She paused, waiting for his reaction.

He leaned back in his chair and folded his hands across his stomach. "Abigail, I realize that you were put in a difficult position, but do not make a rash decision. You've known Robert for most of your life. Though he may not have turned out to be the prince from one of your silly fairy tales, he is from a good family and will take care of you." He paused. "I don't wish to sound unkind, but you must face reality. If you break off your engagement, it is not likely that you will receive another offer."

With unnecessary force, she bit down on her lips to prevent her true feelings about Robert from escaping. "I am prepared to face any future that does not include Robert as my husband, even if it means being alone." Glancing down briefly, she raised her eyes and met Papa's. "Did you know that he has already taken on another mistress?"

His brows rose, indicating that he had not.

Abigail crossed her arms. "A prudent man would

proceed with more caution."

"Your mind is made up, then?"

She nodded. "Yes, Papa. I am sorry to disappoint you, but I'm afraid the circumstances have created an insurmountable void between us."

"Very well. I shall speak with Lord Wrexham." He leafed through the papers on his desk, which was usually a sign of dismissal, but she wasn't finished yet.

Taking a deep breath, she forged on. "Papa, if it is all the same to you, I wish to speak with Robert myself."

"Are you certain that is wise?"

Surely he did not believe Robert would harm her. He would not have attempted to persuade her to continue the engagement if he did. "I believe he deserves an explanation from me."

He nodded once. "I prefer that he call on you here."

"Of course, Papa. I expect him to call at any moment to share his good fortune since he has no reason to suspect the news has already reached me." And if he thought there was any chance of her continuing their engagement, should she not have been the first person he wanted to share the good news with?

She rushed over and hugged Papa. "Thank you for allowing me to cry off and not forcing me to go through with the marriage. I know this is not what you wanted."

He rubbed her back. "I'm sorry I was so fierce when you broached the topic before. I didn't realize that your feelings for Robert had changed so drastically. I thought you were just overreacting to the situation."

"It's all right. You were correct to make me uphold the engagement until Robert's name was cleared."

Abigail headed to her bedchamber to prepare for her impending visit from Robert. It was up to him to seek her out; she would not summon him. Focusing on a book was out of the question. She flopped onto the bed next to Baxter and idly stroked his fur.

A knock sounded on her door. She inhaled deeply and stood. Before she reached the door, it swung open and her mother entered the chamber.

"Darling, come. Sit with me." Mama took her hand and led her back to the bed. "Your father has informed me that you have decided to break your engagement to Lord Hinsdale. I have come to persuade you not to do it."

"May I ask why?"

Patting Abigail's hand, she said, "I realize that things have not turned out the way you envisioned, but that doesn't mean that a happy ending is not still within reach now that you are assured that he is not a murderer."

"Just because he isn't a murderer does not mean he is a desirable husband."

"Yes, your father mentioned your dismay at discovering he has already taken another mistress."

Heat rushed to her face, but she nodded.

"And you know something of what occurs between a man and a woman in the bedchamber, yes?"

If Mama continued in this vane Abigail would burst into flames and burn down the entire house. Gulping for air, she said, "Yes, Mama."

"For some women, performing marital duties becomes an undesirable task. But if a man has a mistress to take care of his base urges, his wife may cease receiving his attentions once she has produced an heir or two."

"I don't think—"

"Bear with me a bit longer. It's not as if having a mistress is unusual, though I will admit one would think Robert might have waited a bit longer before jumping back into the fire." She waved a hand in the air. "Surely he can control himself for more than a few weeks. Especially considering he was accused of murder, for heaven's sake."

"Mother, did you have a point?"

"Just that your aunt and uncle have such an arrangement, and it works very well for them. Once your cousins were born, your aunt was happy to have your uncle pawing at someone else instead of her."

"Mother!" She was in real danger of spontaneously combusting. A desperate glance about the room did not reveal a water pitcher.

"Of course, you know your father has never had a mistress and we are quite happy together, but to each his own. I've never minded your father's attentions. In fact, I look forward to them."

She clapped her hands over her ears as wildly inappropriate images of Mama and Papa attempted to invade her mind. "Please. Stop." Sucking in short, deep breaths, Abigail opened her eyes and focused her gaze out the window. "Please. I cannot…"

"But you must think about it, dear. What if you cry off with Lord Hinsdale and never receive another offer?"

"I am willing to take the risk. There is no longer a way for me to be happy with him."

Mama stood and approached her, leaning over to place a kiss on her forehead. "Very well, my dear. I shall apply myself to the task of finding other prospects for you."

After the door closed behind her mother, Abigail flopped back onto her bed. The woman was not one to give up easily. But really, she could never condone her husband having a mistress. Nowhere in any of her fairy tales was there mention of the hero taking on a mistress to spare his wife the burden of his company. If that was what marriage meant, then perhaps she would be better off alone. Baxter nudged her hand. Rolling onto her stomach, she scratched behind his ears. "At least I know you will always love me. You would never look for another mistress, would you?" He licked her hand and she made a futile wish that a man could be as devoted to her as her dog. Didn't she deserve to marry someone who would love her? Was that too much to ask?

A vision of Edmund popped into her head. He was her idea of what a husband should be, but unfortunately, to him, she might simply be his sister's friend. Of course he liked her, maybe even thought her attractive, but did he love her? They had nearly kissed twice, but she had begun to wonder if he had just been caught up in the excitement of solving the murder. He had to realize that a relationship with her could negatively impact his entire family, and with six unwed sisters, it was a serious concern.

Baxter settled next to her on the bed and she reached for the book that lay open on her pillow, *Beauty and the Beast*. As she immersed herself in the story, she couldn't help but compare Robert unfavorably with the beast. No matter how horrid his behavior during the story, the beast never once considered getting a mistress when Beauty refused his advances, and he certainly didn't rush off to find one as soon as she accepted his proposal.

Lost in the story, it took a moment for the firm knocking

at her door to register. A quick glance at the clock on her mantel revealed that several hours had passed.

Judith entered her chamber. "We must make you presentable. Lord Hinsdale awaits you in the parlor."

Apprehension clawed Abigail's stomach. Their meeting would be unpleasant, but the sooner she ended her engagement with Robert, the better. She sat and slid off the bed, heading for the chair so Judith could repair her hair.

Working quickly, Judith smoothed her hair and added a few pins. All too soon, it was time to go.

"Thank you, Judith." Feeling as if she was being led to the hangman's noose, she traversed the corridor and headed down the staircase to the parlor. A footman stood guard outside the door, and Papa was within, speaking with Robert. The men rose when she entered.

Robert kissed her hand in greeting.

"I believe I shall take my leave. You two have much to discuss." Papa squeezed her arm as he passed by. As his footsteps retreated down the corridor, she sat in a chair and noted that the footman remained just outside the door. Though she was grateful for Papa's forethought and concern, it was a bit daunting that he thought Robert might become angry enough that she would need the aid of a footman.

Robert's face was alight with happiness, and for a moment, she allowed herself to mourn the boy she used to know.

Kneeling before her, he clasped both of her hands, his thumbs caressing her knuckles. A gesture that once had sent excitement through her now elicited only revulsion. "Abigail, the most extraordinary thing has happened. The runner received an anonymous tip last night, and Jane's maid has confessed to orchestrating Sarah's murder."

Pulling her hands from his, she said, "Yes, I've heard. I rather expected a visit from you this morning to share the news."

A flash of anger shone in his eyes. "Who told you?"

"Does it matter?" Biting her lip, she plunged on. "The fact that sharing your news with me wasn't the first thing you did is rather telling, don't you think?"

He stood. "What do you mean?"

"Robert, I was to be your wife. Don't you think proof of your innocence is something you should share with me? That I should have been one of the first to know?"

Crossing his arms, he said, "I don't understand the problem. I'm here now, with the express purpose of telling you just that."

She narrowed her eyes. "When were you informed of the confession?"

"Early this morning."

"And what have you been doing since then?"

Color flooded his face, leaving furious red patches on his neck. "I am not required to justify my whereabouts to you."

She stood and placed her hands on her hips. "No, you are not. But if we were to marry, I would certainly expect a level of deference that has not been present in our relationship."

He took a step toward her. "If we were to be married?"

Clasping her hands in front of her, she said, "Robert, I do not think it is in either of our best interests to continue our engagement."

"What are you saying?"

Though it was perfectly clear to her, he was being deliberately obtuse. "I do not wish to become your wife."

He ran his fingers through his hair, his face suffused with

equal parts heat and anger. "You promised to stand by me. Does your word mean nothing to you?"

It was a low blow, but she attempted to rein in her anger. "I have honored my word. I vowed to stand by you until the investigation ended, and I have done so. I no longer believe we are well suited and wish to cry off."

"You made a promise to me when you agreed to be my wife. I will not allow you to cuckold me."

"Is there any point to hashing things out in this manner?"

"I believe you owe me an explanation."

"Very well." She sat in her chair and indicated with her hand that he should take the settee. "I was devastated when I found out that you had a mistress. And poor Sarah was gone a mere week or two before you replaced her with another woman."

He leapt off the settee and pointed a finger at her. "It is my right as a man to conduct myself as I see fit. Whether or not I choose to have a mistress is none of your affair."

"And that is why I am crying off. I do not wish to wed a man who does not consider me as a partner, as someone who shares every facet of his life."

He took a step closer and she pushed herself against the back of the chair, as far from him as possible. "I think you're being unrealistic. This is life, not one of those fairy tales you've always been so fond of. As my wife, you belong to me and you will do as I say."

She most certainly did not belong to him. "Robert, continuing this conversation is a waste of time for both of us. I no longer want to be your wife. I wish you well." She stood and paced toward the corridor. A vise-like hand clamped over her upper arm and she cried out. The footman moved into the threshold and Robert shot him a glance before leaning close and whispering, "This isn't over. You made a promise and I intend to hold you to it."

Icy slivers of fear stabbed her as he strode from the room.

Chapter Sixteen

Though she was expected at the Trueton ball that evening, Abigail decided she should give Robert time to accept her decision and allow the gossip to quiet before she appeared in public. After dashing off a quick note to let Georgiana know that she shouldn't expect to see her that evening, she found herself with nothing to occupy her. It was impossible to focus on her book. Reading a fairy tale when she was so far from having her own happy ending wasn't a comfort.

Baxter nudged her hand and wagged his tail, his signal that he wanted to go outside. Perhaps a walk in the garden would settle her nerves. After wrapping a shawl around her shoulders, she pulled on her half boots and headed for the staircase with Baxter bounding ahead of her.

Mama emerged from her chamber just as they reached the top step. "Darling, are you certain you don't wish to join us this evening?"

"Yes, Mama. I'm positive. I need to give the gossips time

to grow tired of talking about me before I go out."

Pulling her into a hug, Mama said, "Do not despair. A broken engagement is not such a rare occurrence. They shall soon find a new subject to discuss."

After seeing her parents to the door, she took Baxter out and explored the garden. A footman had already lit the lanterns for them. Hoping to make herself tired enough to sleep, she took several laps around the garden and stayed outside much longer than she normally did.

Stifling a yawn, she whistled to Baxter and headed for her chamber.

Judith was already there, laying out her night rail. "I thought you might want to make an early night of it."

She squeezed her maid's hand. "You know me well."

Judith helped her undress and Abigail pulled on her night rail. "Thank you, Judith."

Once the door clicked closed behind her, Abigail brushed out her hair and braided it quickly before settling on the bed with Baxter at her side. As always, her mind immediately conjured up an image of Edmund. She longed to see him again, but she no longer had the excuse of the investigation to warrant a visit. Though she did not wish to bring any negative attention to his family, perhaps there was a chance for them to be together once some time had passed and the scandal surrounding Robert was eclipsed by another event. It was a comforting thought.

She lowered the lamp on the table next to her bed and settled in, thoroughly exhausted by the events of the day and hoping that sleep might include dreams of Edmund.

• • •

Still holding his empty brandy glass, Edmund glanced at the table where Hinsdale was rapidly becoming inebriated. It seemed an odd way to celebrate his exoneration. The club was unusually quiet this evening. Since Abigail had sent Georgiana a note stating that she would not be attending the Trueton ball, they hadn't stayed long. He had escorted his sister home and headed for White's. Hinsdale had attended briefly as well, but there hadn't been any gossip at the ball about Abigail breaking her engagement with him. However, there had been plenty of chatter about Hinsdale not being guilty of the murder of his mistress.

The same was true at White's. Edmund checked the betting book. The bet over the murder had been settled in the book, but there was nothing about the broken engagement. A wager about whether the couple would reconcile was to be expected if word had gotten out.

Oakley stopped beside him and tapped the page. "Does it seem odd to you that no one has raised the bet about whether Lady Abigail will break the engagement? After all of the scrutiny Hinsdale has exposed her to, I would not blame her for crying off."

"Neither would I," he ground out. Perhaps sensing his mood, Oakley moved off to bother someone else.

The fact that no one seemed to be aware of their broken engagement was bothersome. Perhaps Abigail had decided not to cry off since Hinsdale wasn't guilty. The mere thought created a hollow space inside him and caused him to wave for his brandy to be refilled. Though Hinsdale might not be guilty of murder, he had certainly shown that he was not the most honorable of men. Edmund glanced at him again. Drunk and angry was never a good combination.

Edmund rubbed his forehead. He had unintentionally allowed himself to become embroiled in Abigail's situation. There were already far too many females in his life. Instead of keeping his focus on his family, as he ought to have done, he had allowed himself to care for a woman who read fairy tales and believed in true love, which did not exist.

Perhaps it was for the best she stay with Hinsdale, as she could not be meant for him. All he needed was a bit of time and distance and the emptiness inside him would go away.

Hinsdale downed yet another drink, then stood and headed for the door, likely off to visit his mistress. A footman returned with another glass of brandy, blocking his view of the door. By the time he moved off, Hinsdale was gone. Unease pricked his neck. What if his mistress wasn't the woman he sought? The man was well into his cups. Shoving his chair back, he raced for the door. There was no time to wait for his curricle if he was to follow. He would return for it once he determined that Hinsdale wasn't about to do something stupid.

The startled butler held out his cloak. Tearing it from the man's hands, he raced to the street, but there was no sign of him. "I must speak with Lord Hinsdale. Do you know which direction he went?" Edmund called to the butler.

"I believe he went to the north, my lord."

"Very good." He took off up the street and caught a glimpse of Hinsdale ahead. Forcing himself to slow his steps so he would not be caught following, he hung back while keeping him in sight. One thing was certain. He was not headed in the direction of his own lodgings.

Suddenly, a man rushed across the street and stopped directly in front of Hinsdale. Edmund halted and pretended to be studying the numbers on the houses.

The man took a fistful of Hinsdale's coat. "You've got some nerve leaving my sister to answer for your crimes."

"Unhand me at once." Hinsdale shoved at the man and he let go, but did not give any ground. "I think you have mistaken me for someone else. Clearly you are in the wrong part of town."

"It is you who are mistaken if you think you can get away with having Mary take the blame for you. You told her you would protect her and make sure she got the job as your sister's maid if she figured out a way to get rid of the other girl."

So that was why Hinsdale was so off-kilter. He ought to have known better than to attempt to play women against one another.

Hinsdale took a step back. "I am not to blame for your sister's actions. I may have said something about needing a new mistress if Sarah ever decided to leave, but I never made any promises."

"That's not what Mary said."

"I am done speaking with you. Get out of my way or I'll make sure you and your sister are both implicated." He shoved the man to the side and continued up the street in the opposite direction of his rented rooms.

"Lord Longcroft?"

Damn and blast. The woman had rushed to her front stoop to catch him. Did she have nothing more important to do? "Lady Trington. How…surprising to see you."

The door behind her creaked further open and Lord Trington stuck his head out. "My dear, what are you doing on the…oh. Longcroft."

"Trington." He nodded and risked a glance down the road. Hinsdale was nowhere to be seen.

Lady Trington followed his eyes down the street. "What are you doing so far afield at this time of night?"

Edmund searched his brain for a plausible excuse. Wisbect's house was near, and he had been at White's earlier. "Lord Wisbect left his quizzing glass at the club, and it's such a fine night, I thought I'd return it before heading home."

Trington nodded, though his wife still eyed him suspiciously. "If you'll excuse me, I must hurry before he retires for the evening."

"Of course, my lord." Lady Trington forged on with her agenda. "Will we have the pleasure of your company at Lady Mary's coming out ball next week?"

"I'm afraid I shall have to defer to Lady Georgiana's wishes, but it is a distinct possibility." He glanced down the street again. At this point, his only option was to go to Jaffrey House and make sure Hinsdale was not there.

"If you'll excuse me, I must continue on my errand." He bowed and charged down the street, heedless of their farewells.

The hair rose on the back of his neck as he realized the direction Hinsdale had taken. He was headed to Abigail's house. Of course, because he needed her to marry him to offset any scandal the maid and her family might cause while trying to implicate him in the murder.

• • •

Baxter's low growl startled Abigail from a deep sleep.

The lamp by her bed revealed the outline of a man

climbing through her window. Stifling a scream, she scrambled to turn up the lamp.

Baxter snapped his jaws as Robert stalked toward her bed.

She yanked the bedclothes up to her shoulders. "Robert, what are you doing? I insist you leave my chamber at once."

In the dim light, his eyes gleamed like a feral animal. "I think not, my dear. Tonight I am going to make you mine, and you will have no choice but to go through with our marriage."

As he came closer to the bed, Baxter lunged at him. Abigail grabbed his collar just in time to keep him from leaping off the bed at Robert.

"Control that mongrel or I'll snap its neck."

Clutching Baxter to her, she pulled him into her lap to quiet him. She narrowed her eyes at Robert. "This is outrageous behavior. If you don't leave my chamber at once, I shall cry out and half of the household will come running."

He leaned against the post at the foot of her bed and crossed his arms. "Go ahead. It would make my plans much easier to enact. Once others witness my presence in your chamber, you shall have to marry me or be ruined."

The odor of spirits and stale cigars wafted over her and she gagged. *Damnation*! He was correct. "Robert, you are drunk and not in your right mind. Leave. Now."

Of course he didn't listen. As he confidently sauntered toward her, she scrambled to her feet and kept her dog behind her. Robert would have to go through her to get to Baxter.

In a flash, he clamped onto her wrist and twisted her arm behind her back. With his other hand, he cupped her breast.

Fear and outrage mingled in her veins, and she smashed her forehead against his nose as her brother had taught her.

"You bitch." He put one hand to his nose and grabbed her braid with the other, yanking her onto her knees.

Tears formed in her eyes, threatening to fall. Before she could react, he ripped the front of her night rail in one swift movement, but the thick placket halted the tear before it reached her breasts.

Ignoring the pain in her scalp, she used both hands to hold her night rail together. "Robert, this is beyond foolish. You could be prosecuted for this behavior. Leave now or I will call for help."

"I grow weary of your idle threats." After taking a deep breath, he reached out and wiped away her tears with the pad of his thumb, suddenly gentle. "It doesn't have to be this way between us. You remember how close we once were. Marry me and all will be forgiven."

He swayed and let go of her hair in favor of steadying himself against the bed post. Quickly grabbing her shawl to cover herself, she sat on the bed in front of Baxter and studied him. As before, he exhibited a confusing mix of hot and cold behavior toward her. Which Robert would appear next?

"I'm glad you've finally seen reason. That excuse for a dog needs to get off the bed. Put him in your dressing room and I will show you how things can be between us." He tried to caress her cheek with the back of his hand, but she dodged out of reach and swung Baxter around behind her, her back to the window.

Robert frowned. "I thought I told you to lock that dog in your dressing room." Before she could react, he made a grab for Baxter's collar. Robert roared as Baxter's teeth sank into his wrist. Her dog yelped in pain when Robert's foot connected with his stomach. He grabbed Baxter by the scruff of his neck and began dragging him toward the window. Abigail jumped onto Robert's back and wrapped her arms around his throat, but he shook her off. Baxter whimpered and twisted as Robert towed him to the window.

• • •

As Edmund rounded the corner toward Jaffrey House, he noted that the lanterns were lit at the front of the house, but the rooms on the second floor were all dark. Lord and Lady Jaffrey must not have returned from the ball. Having no idea where Abigail's chamber was, he dashed around the side of the house. Light shone from a single, open window. The faint cries of a dog reached him, followed by an angry male voice that sounded like Hinsdale, and a moment later, Abigail's form moved past the window.

Having fallen from a tree and broken his arm when he was but six years old, he was not fond of heights. He studied the tree that Hinsdale must have climbed to get to her chamber. It seemed sturdy enough, but perhaps it would be faster to pound on the front door and demand admittance. Except then every servant in the household would bear witness to Robert's presence in Abigail's bedchamber. She would be ruined, or worse, forced to marry him.

There was no choice but to climb the tree, and there was no time to lose. Grasping a low, thick branch, he pulled himself up. He ascended quickly until he made the mistake of looking down and the ground shifted beneath him. Closing his eyes and sucking in a breath, he continued, ignoring the cold sweat covering him. The dog had ceased growling. His whimpers melded with Abigail's cries.

Redoubling his efforts, he gripped the window sill and was about to climb through when something smashed into his shoulder. Purely by reflex, he let go of the sill and grabbed for what turned out to be the dog. Steadying himself against the trunk of the tree, he cradled the dog against his chest.

"How could you," Abigail cried. She shoved Robert away and leaned out the window.

"Edmund?" The moonlight illuminated the worry in her eyes.

"Your dog is safe. Move back so we can enter." Leaning against the sill, he lifted the dog through and into Abigail's waiting arms. While swinging his leg over, he had to squelch the urge to kick Hinsdale, who stood as if in a stupor. Until Edmund's feet hit the floor.

"What are you about, Longcroft? What happens between me and my intended is none of your affair, and you have no right to enter her bedchamber."

"You have no right to be here, either. Lady Abigail broke off her engagement with you, so she is not your intended." At least he hoped she had. He glanced at her, but she had dropped to the floor, examining her dog for injuries.

Hinsdale straightened his shoulders. "That was a misunderstanding, one which I intend to remedy."

Meeting Robert's gaze with her own glare, she said, "There is no misunderstanding. Get out of my chamber. Now. I hope never to see you again."

Hinsdale reached down and ran his finger across her lips, and it was all Edmund could do not to smash his fist into the bastard's face.

She swatted at his hand. "Do not touch me. Get out."

The door shot open and slammed against the wall. Abigail jumped to her feet.

Lord Jaffrey stood in the doorway, his face resembling the hue of a ripe strawberry. "Hinsdale! Longcroft! Why are in you in my daughter's bedchamber?"

Abigail rushed into her father's embrace.

Hinsdale placed a hand against his head and closed his eyes, leaving Edmund to answer.

But Abigail found words before he did. "Papa, Robert came in through my window. I believe his intention was to convince me to marry him, but he is drunk. When Baxter tried to defend me, he threw him out the window." She sucked in a shuddering breath and continued. "I don't know how or why, but Lord Longcroft was attempting to enter through the window at that exact moment and he caught Baxter."

Lady Jaffrey, the butler, and numerous other staff had gathered behind Abigail and her father. This was not good at all.

"I don't care why they are here. They have put you and all of us in a very difficult position." He glanced into the corridor and blanched. "Williams, please escort everyone below stairs. I do not wish to have an audience while I sort this out."

The butler went to work herding the staff away from the door. Only Lord and Lady Jaffrey remained.

Lord Jaffrey leveled his stare at Hinsdale. "Hinsdale, what were you thinking?"

He had the sense to look sheepish. Or perhaps the

alcohol had caught up with him. Either way, he was blessedly silent.

"Never mind. We have a problem now. Not one, but two bachelors are in my daughter's bedchamber." He glanced at the floor and back up again, meeting first Edmund's then Hinsdale's eyes.

"One of you is going to have to marry her."

"I will." It slipped out of Edmund's mouth without thought.

Hinsdale finally came out of his stupor. "Like hell you will. She will marry me."

Jaffrey rounded on him. "You had your chance, Hinsdale. There isn't the slightest possibility that she'll agree to marry you after you tried to throw her dog out the window."

Hinsdale scowled but didn't argue, perhaps realizing for the first time that it really was over for him with Abigail.

Abigail looked stricken. She glanced at him, then back to her father. "Papa, please. This isn't necessary."

"It sure as hell is." He waved a hand toward Edmund. "Longcroft, call on me tomorrow to discuss the settlements." Taking a step into the corridor, he bellowed, "Williams."

He materialized as if he had been waiting to be summoned, which he probably had been. "Yes, my lord?"

Jaffrey pointed at Hinsdale. "Remove this man from the premises."

"Yes, my lord." He wrestled Hinsdale out the door and proceeded to push him down the corridor.

"Wait." Jaffrey closed his eyes and rubbed his temples. "Have the carriage brought around and instruct the coachman to drop him off at Wrexham House. He can explain this chaos to his father."

Abigail grasped her father's arm. "Papa, please don't force Lord Longcroft to marry me."

He placed his palm against her cheek and met her eyes. "Darling, it is the only way to salvage this situation. Would you rather marry Hinsdale?"

"No!"

"Then Longcroft it is." He glanced at Edmund and said, "Now I must go threaten the servants with dismissal if we have any hope of keeping tonight's events private."

After watching her father leave, Abigail finally turned and approached him, her expression shuttered. "Lord Longcroft, I cannot thank you enough for saving Baxter."

Tucking a loose strand of hair behind her ear, he said, "Under the circumstances, I think you should call me Edmund." The dog moved from her side and sat on his foot as if expressing his gratitude as well. Edmund knelt beside him and rubbed his ears, earning a lick of regard.

Abigail pulled in a shuddering breath. "I will be forever grateful to you for rescuing both me and Baxter." She wrapped her hands in the folds of her gown before continuing. "I'm so sorry you've been forced to—"

"I have not been forced to do anything." Taking a step toward her, he drew her hands to his mouth and pressed a kiss into her palm. "I came here of my own accord because I was concerned for your safety." He watched her face as he kissed the other palm. Her eyes widened and a charming blush crept up her neck. "And no one coerced me to marry you."

"My father certainly—"

He effectively quieted her protests by placing a finger against her lips. "Your father cannot force me to do something

I do not want to do. If you don't wish to marry me, that is one thing, but do not mistake my intentions."

She stared at him, and he wished he could read her thoughts. Did she really not want to marry him, or was she upset that he appeared not to have had any say in the matter? These were things they could explore in the morning, when they had both had a chance to rest.

He led her toward her bed, which Baxter gladly jumped upon. "I think he's trying to tell you something," he said, nodding at the dog.

She shot him the first smile he had seen from her since entering her room.

"It is time for all of us to get some sleep. I will call on you tomorrow." He kissed her forehead and strode from the room before she could formulate more protests.

Chapter Seventeen

Normally an early riser, Abigail woke long after the sun came up and wondered why no one had disturbed her. The events of the previous night slammed into her, robbing her of breath. Robert really had tried to kill Baxter, and she had trapped Edmund into marrying her. Since Baxter was not to be found, she concluded that Judith had snuck in earlier to take him out.

Leaping from the bed, she moved to the window and noted that the Longcroft carriage sat in front of the mews. Before she awoke, she had been having a lovely dream about Edmund proposing to her voluntarily because he was in love with her and not because he had been forced by circumstances to marry her. A desperate giggle escaped her lips. If it weren't so awful, it would have been funny. She could picture the scene in her bedchamber drawn out on a scandal sheet. Her father, larger than life, looming over Robert and Edmund, insisting one of them had to marry her as they exchanged desperate glances, each hoping the other would step up.

After allowing herself a deep sigh, she rang for Judith and rushed to scour her dressing room for something to wear. It seemed too much to hope that a gown had magically appeared overnight that said I'm-sorry-I-trapped-you-into-marriage-but-won't-you-please-love-me-anyway. After all, it had been proven on multiple occasions that her life certainly was not a fairy tale. Edmund had swept in and rescued her in the tradition of a fairy tale prince, but could he love her? She wasn't sure precisely when it had happened, but she was in love with him. She recognized the feeling, because it was something that she had never felt for Robert.

But since she did love him, she also recognized that the best thing for her to do was release him from any obligation to her. Georgiana and the rest of his sisters did not deserve to be affected by her past, even if Edmund was willing to weather the inevitable storm.

Mama had begun to let her chose bolder colors after her second year out, but neither blue nor lavender seemed right. Bold was not the image she wished to project. Calm and controlled was more what she wanted. Perhaps the green silk. Understated but elegant.

The door clicked and she turned just in time to grasp Baxter's front feet as he bounced up to lick her face.

Judith entered behind him, her expression contrite. "I'm so sorry I wasn't here to assist you last night. Had I been present, you would not have been forced to marry Lord Longcroft."

Abigail placed a hand on her maid's shoulder. "There was no way for you, or anyone else for that matter, to know that Lord Hinsdale would behave in such a manner. You mustn't upset yourself." And it wasn't as if having to marry Edmund was a bad thing for her.

Turning back to the closet, she said, "Rather than thinking overmuch about my situation, we shall focus on the things we can control, such as what I should wear today. What do you think of the green silk for my first official meeting with my intended?"

"Shall I fetch your emerald necklace and ear bobs?"

Abigail nodded. "Yes. There is nothing like jewelry to boost one's confidence."

Judith helped her don her underclothes and gown in silence, then swept her hair into a simple but elegant twist. There was nothing left for her to do but go to the parlor and wait for her father to finish his meeting with Edmund. She called to Baxter and headed for the staircase.

Edmund had been utterly charming last night, and if he had made an offer for her under normal circumstances, she would have been ecstatic. But how was he feeling about his situation under the scrutiny of the bright light of day? Though she wished to pace across the parlor, the door was open, so she forced herself to sit like a lady and pretend to be occupied with her sketch book. After flipping past several unfinished designs, she knew the focus she required to draw would be elusive.

Just when she thought she might go mad with waiting, footsteps sounded in the corridor. Papa entered, followed closely by Edmund. His countenance revealed no hint as to the direction of his thoughts.

"Darling." Papa walked over and kissed her on the cheek. "We have been through all of the settlements." He waved a hand for them to sit. Abigail returned to the settee, and Edmund chose the seat next to her.

"Longcroft and I agree that it would be best to postpone the wedding for a time. Though there has been no sign that the events of last night are known outside of this house, we think it best for both of you to stay out of society until the news of your broken engagement with Hinsdale is eclipsed by some other bit of gossip. Then we will announce your engagement."

"Yes, Papa." She hazarded a glance at Edmund, but his expression remained neutral. Her stomach clenched. He must regret the chivalrous impulse that spurred him to offer for her last night.

Papa stood. "Now that everything is settled, I'm going to call on Lord Wrexham. There's no way to know what version of last night's events he has been given, and I want to make certain he knows the truth."

Turning to Edmund, he said, "Welcome to the family, son."

Edmund stood and shook his hand, then watched as Papa exited the parlor and shut the door behind him.

Surprise and regret swirled tempestuously in Abigail's stomach as the realization that she was truly engaged to Edmund hit her yet again. She stood and bowed her head. "My lord, please allow me to apologize again for the situation you now find yourself in."

"Abigail, stop apologizing. And if you don't stop being so formal with me, I shall have to come up with a suitable punishment to remind you."

Whipping her face up to meet his eyes, the laughter she spotted dancing there dispelled her fleeting concern that he was serious. "I am prepared to cry off as soon as things have settled down and there is a new scandal to occupy society. Perhaps after…"

"You've given me no choice. I shall have to commence with the torture after all." He stopped inches from her, his warm breath ruffling her hair. He ran the pad of his thumb along her jaw and followed her pulse down to the edge of her collar bone. Awash in sensation, she allowed her eyes to close and her lips to part, needing the air to steady herself.

Just when she had decided to open her eyes, his finger traced her lips, sending shockwaves through her. Then his mouth brushed over hers and she grasped his shoulders to keep from swooning.

He pulled away and she opened her eyes to his smiling face. "I see my methods have been successful."

"But I—"

"No more talk of crying off. Your father and I have already decided that our best course of action is to lie low until we are certain that Hinsdale will cause us no problems. Then we shall quietly announce our engagement to a few influential members of society and begin going out in society together."

"But—"

He pressed his finger against her mouth.

"There are no buts. If you still don't wish to marry me after we've carried out our plan, I will allow you to cry off. But not now. Not while your reputation is still at stake."

She turned away from him, frightened of the intensity in his eyes. "My lord, it's not that I don't want to—"

Grasping her shoulders, he turned her to face him and placed quick kisses up her neck before capturing her mouth. He pulled her tight against him, their bodies melding together in all the right places. A frisson shot through her and she leaned more tightly against him. His tongue slid along the seam of her lips and they parted as if of their own accord, allowing him in. She sighed when he finally pulled away.

"I hope you've learned your lesson. It's Edmund. Or if you prefer, you may devise a pet name for me. But if you refer to me as 'my lord' one more time, I shall not be held responsible for my actions."

Having become accustomed to his serious nature, his playfulness threw her off balance. "Of course, my—" Just as his shoulders tensed, she stopped her wayward tongue, though there was a part of her that was *very* curious about what his next lesson would entail. "Edmund."

"That's better." He sent her a tentative smile. "I haven't had a chance to share our good news with my family. Would you care to accompany me to Longcroft Hall?"

Abigail's skin went cold. What would his family think when they found out she had trapped him into marriage? What would Georgiana say? How much of the story did he plan to tell them? She swallowed and marshaled a response. "Do you think it wise to have me with you when you break the news?"

He clasped her hands in his warm grip and looked into her eyes. "Abigail, you must stop viewing our betrothal in such a negative light. Regardless of how it came about, it is an event to be celebrated, not feared."

She prayed that he couldn't feel the trembling of her fingers. "What will we tell them? Surely they will deduce that something unusual has transpired. At this time yesterday, I was still betrothed to another man."

He sighed. "Georgiana will be the problem. No one else will be impolite enough to question my decision."

"Perhaps you should speak with her alone. I will not be able to stand up to her questioning and will reveal the entire story."

He squeezed her hands and let them go. Turning toward the window, he said, "I suppose you are right. It is not fair of me to use you to deflect questions from my family. He turned back to her. "There will be gossip and speculation about our engagement. Though I wish the circumstances could be kept between us, it is unlikely. It is best that at least Georgiana and Henrietta know the truth so they can help deflect any malicious gossip."

Abigail nodded in agreement. She still thought it would be better for him and his family if she cried off now, but he had made it clear that he would not allow it. "I expect Georgiana to appear on my doorstep the moment you tell her."

"I fear you are correct. I will urge her to channel her excess energy into making the arrangements for a private dinner with you and your family so everyone can get to know you better."

"It's not as if they don't already know me."

"True, but they know you as Georgiana's friend, not my future wife."

Her stomach jumped at the possessive tone in his voice. It was possible that he was fond of her, but would it be enough to sustain a marriage? Would it break her heart to love him if he wouldn't, couldn't return her feelings?

• • •

As he walked the short distance to Longcroft Hall, Edmund contemplated Abigail's hesitation to embrace their alliance. After all, he had no idea how she really felt about him. She had been trapped into marriage just as much as he had, and he certainly was not the hero from one of her fairy tales. Her reservations could be many. He didn't believe in love, and he was more interested in mathematical calculations than society events.

Though he certainly had never imaged he would wind up betrothed to Abigail, he was not displeased with the match. She was a beautiful, sensible woman from a good family. Despite his vow not to marry until at least some of his sisters had been situated, he found himself looking forward to having her by his side to help negotiate the treacherous waters of the marriage mart with his sisters. The only reservation he harbored was whether he could make her happy, considering that he certainly would not measure up to her fictional heroes. Still, they would get on well together, and that was more than many couples could claim. He would have to work to convince her that he wasn't a dolt who was only interested in mathematics and science, but that he truly wanted to marry her.

Whistling as he entered his home, he smiled at Woolford and handed him his hat and top coat. "Please send for Henrietta immediately and inform Georgiana that she is wanted in my study."

"Very well, my lord."

Woolford worked so quickly, Georgiana met him in

the threshold of his study. She must have come from the breakfast room. "Good morning." He held his arm out and ushered her in.

Georgiana narrowed her eyes. "What has you in such good spirits this morning?"

"I have news to share, but we must wait for Henrietta to arrive. You are familiar with my dislike of repeating myself."

"Then you ought to have waited for her to arrive before summoning me." She plopped down into a chair. "Does it pertain to the murder?"

"Not directly, no."

She tilted her head. He could almost hear her mind working. "You must tell me now or I will die of curiosity."

"I shall miss you." He turned away to look out the window, expecting to be whacked in the head with a projectile at any moment. Rustling sounds ensued, followed by the steady tap of fingers making contact with the top of his desk. Siblings were the worst sort of foes, as they knew all of ones weaknesses.

"Are you hoping to drive me mad, or annoy the information out of me?"

"Either option would please me."

Their stalemate continued until Henrietta arrived a short time later. She swept into the room, eclipsing Woolford's need to announce her.

"I was already on my way here when your footman intercepted me," she said by way of explanation.

Edmund turned from the window. "I have happy news to share. I am betrothed to Abigail."

Georgiana leapt from her chair. "What! When? How?"

Edmund looked to Hen and raised his brows.

"Did she not just break her engagement to Lord Hinsdale?" she asked.

He held a hand out toward the chairs in front of his desk. "Let's get comfortable." He sat behind his desk and debated the wisdom of tying Georgiana down. Staying still was not one of her strong points, and it was difficult to concentrate with her bouncing around.

"Lady Abigail did indeed break off her engagement to Lord Hinsdale. Unfortunately, he was not pleased with her decision. I noted his inebriation and decided to follow him when he left White's last night, and he led me straight to Abigail's bedchamber, where he intended to compromise her so she could not end their engagement."

"But what—"

"Do allow me to finish before you sling questions at me. Without going into too much detail, suffice it to say we are now engaged. Lord Jaffrey has taken every precaution to ensure that the events of last night are not leaked to society, but that will require cooperation from Hinsdale, who, as you know, is unreliable at best."

No longer able to contain his restless energy, he stood and paced behind his desk. "I wanted the two of you to know the real story in case word somehow leaks and we have to present a united front to society. However, I think it best if we keep these circumstances from Mother and the younger girls."

"Yes, of course," said Henrietta. "There is no cause to upset Mother unnecessarily."

"But…never mind. I must speak to Abigail." Georgiana leapt from her chair and headed for the door.

"I believe Abigail already has enough to deal with. You

may direct your questions to me."

Georgiana studied him, her head tilted slightly to the side. "Despite your repeated assertions that you have no desire to marry, you don't seem particularly disturbed by your sudden betrothal."

He rocked back and forth on his feet. "Did you have a question?"

Georgiana rolled her eyes. He glanced to Hen just as she wiped a tear from her cheek. She rushed to him and engulfed him in a hug. "Thank you for coming to Abigail's rescue. I don't think you'll regret your decision."

She pulled back and smiled at him. After calming her sniffles, she said, "However did you get into her chamber?"

"The same way Hinsdale did. I climbed up to the window."

"You what?" Georgiana said.

Hen smiled again. "You must like Abigail very much to have conquered your fear of heights."

"I must admit I find myself content with the situation." That was as much as he would say. Georgiana would hound him tirelessly if he gave away too much.

"Georgiana, I would appreciate it if you could organize a private dinner tomorrow night for Abigail and her parents. It will simply be a small affair between our families so we can become more familiar with one another."

"Very well." Georgiana nodded. "Hen, would you be so kind as to help me plan the menu?"

"Of course."

His sisters took their leave, and he returned to his desk, feeling more content than he had ever been since becoming the head of his family.

Chapter Eighteen

Abigail checked her appearance in the mirror one last time before leaving her bedchamber. Feeling more nervous than she had been when she made her debut, she had been unable even to decide which gown to wear and left the decision to Judith. Repeatedly scolding herself for being a ninny had done nothing to calm her nerves. She was being silly. Everyone at Longcroft Hall already knew her. But Edmund's determination not to marry was well known, even among society. There would be questions, especially from his family. The question that set her nerves on end was whether they would accept her as part of their family after being simply Georgiana's friend for so long.

"Darling, you are gorgeous." Mama hugged her tight. "Why have you not worn this gown before? It flatters your skin tone."

The gown Judith chose was crafted of gold silk overlaid with lace, which she had thought would leave her looking sallow. As such, she wasn't sure if Mama was sincere, or attempting to calm her nerves.

"Can we walk to Longcroft Hall? I haven't been outside all day and would enjoy some fresh air."

Mama exchanged a glance with Papa and nodded. "I suppose so. We can always summon the carriage to bring us home."

Though Abigail didn't share her thoughts, she deemed it better not to leave their carriage visible at Longcroft Hall until after their betrothal had been announced.

The walk to Longcroft Hall passed quickly and in near silence. If it was this awkward with her own parents, how would she fare with Edmund's family?

The butler noted their arrival and ushered them into the house. After divesting themselves of their outerwear, they were led to the parlor, where Edmund's entire family, minus the youngest two girls, stood ready to greet them.

Abigail took a steadying breath. Edmund came to her and took her hand, leading her to his mother. His calm presence served as a balm to her frazzled nerves.

"I know you are already familiar with Abigail, but I wish to introduce her to you as my future wife."

Lady Longcroft squeezed her hand. "I believe you have made a wise choice, Edmund. Anyone able to put up with Georgiana's antics is to be prized."

She moved off to greet Abigail's parents, and Abigail took her first deep breath of the evening.

"I guess that could have been worse."

Edmund stroked his thumb across her palm, sending jolts up her arm. "Aside from your unfortunate association with Hinsdale, your reputation is impeccable. Any mother would be proud to have her son engaged to you." He lifted her hand and kissed her palm, his lips nearly singeing her even through the fabric of her glove. Georgiana rushed over then, and crushed Abigail into a hug. "I could not be happier to have you as a sister." She grasped Abigail's hand and pulled her toward the corner. "Edmund has only shared the barest of details with us. I expect you to call on me tomorrow and provide a complete account of everything that transpired."

Before Abigail could organize her thoughts into a response, Lady Longcroft returned. Both Georgiana and Edmund moved to speak with Papa, and Abigail's feeling of inadequacy resurfaced, strangling her confidence and causing her words of greeting to lodge in her throat.

"Edmund has indicated that you were much thrown together while investigating the death of Lord Wrexham's servant."

"Yes, my lady. He was extremely generous with his time, and in fact helped uncover the murderer."

"Edmund is the best of men, but he has his own priorities and schedule that sometimes does not always mesh with the rest of society. Are you aware that he is often occupied for long periods of time with his experiments?"

"Yes, my lady. Georgiana has frequently shared her frustrations with his absent-mindedness, and of course I have spent a great deal of time here at Longcroft Hall." Abigail clasped her hands tightly, unsure where Lady Longcroft was going with this conversation. "I assure you that I have no intention of disrupting his lordship's schedule." Where had Georgiana gotten to? With nine other people in the room, how had she managed to be alone with Lady Longcroft?

"Are you also aware that he had no intention of marrying

this soon?"

Abigail nodded.

"I have no idea why he changed his mind, but he is devoted to his sisters and intends to see that they all marry well."

"Of course, my lady. I would expect nothing less from him, and hope to be of service in that regard."

"Very well."

She moved away, leaving Abigail wondering if Lady Longcroft would warm to her with time. She really couldn't blame her for being suspicious of the circumstances surrounding their hasty engagement. Despite Edmund's repeated assurances, she had to remember that breaking their engagement might be the correct thing for her to do.

Abigail moved toward Henrietta, whom she had yet to speak with since the announcement.

Henrietta took her hand. "Abigail, I am so glad that Edmund was able to rescue you from Hinsdale. I don't like to think of what might have happened if he hadn't been there."

Noting the tremor in her voice, Abigail put her arm around Henrietta. "He is my prince, my knight who executed a rescue more daring than any I've read about in a book." It was true. He had rescued her in every way there was to be rescued, and she was hopelessly in love with him. Glancing back over her shoulder, she caught him watching her, looking more animated that she had ever seen him. Maybe, just maybe, this was the best thing that had ever happened to either of them.

Chapter Nineteen

The next morning, Abigail wandered about her chamber, finally refreshed and ready to begin the next chapter of her life, and wondering how long an interval would be necessary before they could hold the wedding ceremony. After stretching out the kinks from her deep sleep, she opened her wardrobe and searched for something to wear. Perhaps something yellow to reflect her sunny mood.

Judith burst into the room without knocking, which was generally a sign of an emergency of some sort.

"Lord Longcroft is here and wishes to see you immediately."

Gooseflesh rose on her neck. "Did he say why he wanted to see me?"

"I'm sure I don't know. Williams simply told me to fetch you with haste."

This did not bode well. Edmund was always calm and careful, and this sense of urgency was disconcerting. She yanked the first yellow gown she came across from her wardrobe, though the optimistic mood she had awoken with had disintegrated.

After dressing as if her life depended on her ability to be quick, she descended to the parlor, where she found Edmund pacing impatiently. He ran his eyes over her, then thrust a gossip sheet into her hand. Her stomach dropped to the floor. After the first disastrous information was released about the murder, Abigail had been careful to avoid the gossip sheets whenever possible. It had to be something dire for Edmund to subject her to it. She closed her eyes and took a deep breath before reading it.

> *The maddening silence has finally been broken by Lord H. Lady A cried off from her engagement with Lord H and became betrothed to Lord L less than a day later. Lord H hinted that the hasty engagement was necessary due to a compromising situation. Do not despair, loyal subscribers. This lady intends to investigate further.*

Horror washed over Abigail, robbing her of breath. "How could he?" she whispered.

Edmund paced in front of the closed door. "The bastard. What could he possibly stand to gain from this?"

"Nothing. He seeks revenge." Abigail allowed the numbness to wash over her, welcoming the deadening of her feelings. She knew what she had to do. She would not besmirch Edmund or his family with her scandal. If she broke their engagement, he could emerge from this situation as the hero that he was. He would be credited with saving her from Robert, but would not be brought down by a permanent association with her.

"I am going to cry off. I will not have you or your family tainted by association with me."

"Abigail, I am the Marquess of Longcroft. Considering that the truth of Robert's actions will come out in time, I am not concerned about my reputation or that of my family. We have nothing to hide and will have no trouble weathering this small storm."

He was correct about Robert's actions coming out. Everyone would also learn that Edmund had been forced by his own honor to marry her. But no, it was better to break things off now.

Clearly she could not escape scandal no matter how hard she tried. "Edmund, I must thank you again for coming to my rescue, but I will not hold you to our betrothal. Your chivalrous actions should not require you to be bound to me for all eternity."

She turned away from him to hide her tears, but he would not allow her to escape. He wrapped his hands around her shoulders and gently turned her to face him. He wiped the tears from her face before speaking.

"Abigail, is this what you want? To end our engagement?"

She shuddered. "From the start, none of this has been about what I want."

His features softened, almost as if he was hurt by her words. "So you no longer wish to marry me?"

She wanted to marry him more than anything, but she could not. There would always be gossip and speculation about them no matter how much time passed. It was not fair to submit him, or Georgiana or Elizabeth, to that sort of scrutiny. The only way he could emerge unscathed was if she let him out of his obligation. Allowing him to think she didn't love him was the most efficient way to proceed.

Though it was the hardest thing she had ever done, she lifted her eyes to meet his and lied with a steady voice. "No, I do not want to marry you."

Anguish crossed his face for an instant before it cleared of all emotion. "Very well. I will abide by your wishes, but now that everyone knows we are betrothed, we will have to appear together. I ask only that you wait to share your decision for at least a fortnight, until such a time as the gossip and speculation has been eclipsed by some other scandal."

He turned and strode for the door. Her heart aching, she reached for him, then thought better of it and let him go.

· · ·

Just before dinner, a soft knock sounded on her door. She stood and checked her appearance in the mirror. Too devastated to cry, the only outward sign of her heartbreak was her pale countenance. The blessed numbness that had overcome her earlier persisted. She opened the door to her father.

"Darling, I've come with an update from Wrexham. He has exiled Hinsdale back to the continent. He is to leave tomorrow and not return for at least a year." He looked closely at her face and chucked her under the chin like he had done since she was a little girl.

"Don't worry, my darling. With his absence will come a respite, and you will be able to wed Longcroft soon."

So Edmund had not gone to Papa about their soon to be broken betrothal. If she told him now, he would only attempt to sway her as Edmund had. It was better to wait to break the news to him until Edmund thought it was time it be made public. Though there was nothing else she could do to repair the situation between them, she could allow him that small courtesy.

He pulled her into a hug. "Thank you, Papa," she whispered.

"This will all soon be over, darling, and you can move forward with the rest of your life."

A life she would spend alone.

Chapter Twenty

Having to attend balls and continue the ruse of his betrothal to Abigail was akin to being sent to Dante's Eighth Circle of hell. Edmund was a fraud. As far as he knew, Abigail and he were the only ones who were aware that she had cried off. Though he had assumed she would at least tell Georgiana, she had not, and he would not. It was her decision, and therefore her information to share.

He glanced about the ballroom. Thankfully this was a fairly small gathering, which meant fewer people attempting to glean information from them. They both carefully deflected any questions regarding Hinsdale, which wasn't too difficult as his forced exile on the continent was well known among the *ton*. He feared the response once it was known that Abigail had cried off for a second time, especially after Hinsdale had made it known that they had been caught in a compromising position. There would be no damage to his reputation, but Abigail's very well might be irreparable.

So far, their routine had worked brilliantly. By tacit agreement, they arrived fashionably late, danced three sets together to remind everyone of their engagement, then stayed just late enough not to draw attention.

He spotted her across the room, looking as beautiful and elegant as ever in a blue gown that made her eyes sparkle. Skirting the perimeter of the dance floor, he weaved his way through the crowd and stopped next to Abigail.

"My lady," he said, and kissed her hand, something he would never have done in public, except to a lady to whom he was betrothed. He hadn't known the depths of his acting skills until the need had arose to become a master of deception.

"Good evening, my lord."

"Would you care to dance?"

She nodded and he led her onto the floor to take up position for a waltz. They turned to face one another, and he took both of her hands, absently stroking across her knuckles with his thumbs. There was a blue tint beneath her eyes and lines of strain at their outside edges, revealing that she might not be as unaffected as he had thought.

Neither of them spoke, and as the music began, she glanced around the ballroom. After a few moments of silence, he asked, "Are you by chance redesigning some poor, unassuming lady's gown?"

"No, I find I don't have the desire to design at present." She kept her eyes carefully trained over his left shoulder. "I thought perhaps you were performing calculations."

"No, I similarly find myself unable to concentrate on such pursuits."

And that was end of their conversation. He pulled her

closer and held her much tighter than was seemly, allowing the warmth of her body to mingle with his, not caring what conclusions their observers drew. He didn't understand what he had done to turn her away, to make a life alone seem more preferable than a life with him, but he would continue to treat her as his intended until she made public her wish to end their association.

• • •

Edmund went to his study as soon as they returned from the ball. He had not been untruthful with Abigail when he said that he no longer seemed to possess a mind for calculations. Instead, he had been singularly focused on finding a formula to prove that love existed. No matter how hard he tried, no amount of calculating the variables amounted to anything. He had been correct. Love did not exist as far as science and reason was concerned.

However, there had to be some explanation for the strong feelings he had for Abigail, feelings that he could not shake. They had to have some basis. He wasn't unfamiliar with being attracted to a woman, but the symptoms he was experiencing went far beyond that. He sat down to make a list of his complaints, which included insomnia, the inability to concentrate, loss of appetite, and if he was completely honest with himself, an increased heartbeat and small pains in the region of his chest.

A knock sounded. "Enter," he said, assuming it was Woolford.

Georgiana flew into the room. "Edmund, what is wrong with you?"

He glanced up from his paper. "I beg your pardon?"

"You and Abigail barely said ten words to one another at the ball." She plunked herself down in the chair in front of his desk.

"You need to speak with Abigail."

"I tried. She was even less forthcoming than you." She leaned closer. "Edmund, what is amiss?"

He leaned back against his chair. "This isn't my information to share. You need to speak to Abigail."

"You're frightening me now." She reached across the desk and covered his hand with hers. "I cannot help if you won't tell me what is happening."

He dropped his head into his hands. Perhaps revealing the secret to someone would ease his mind. "On the day we discovered the scandal sheet, Abigail cried off. I persuaded her to keep that information private for a time, but the fact remains that we are no longer betrothed.

"Why? How?"

He shook his head. "I don't know. I tried to talk her out of it, but she refused to be swayed."

When she failed to respond as he had expected, he looked up to find her reading his list. "What is this?"

"I am attempting to determine what is wrong with me."

She read aloud from his list. "Insomnia, loss of appetite, inability to concentrate." Looking up, she met his eyes. "Sounds to me like you're in love."

"Impossible." He leapt from his chair and paced to the dark window. "I have already determined that love does not exist."

"You're a fool if you think that." The sound of her chair scraping the floor as she stood assaulted his ears. "I take that back. You are a damn fool."

He turned to her, his eyes narrowed.

"Edmund, don't you see? You're in love with her."

He opened his mouth to respond, but she held her hand up for him to be quiet.

"Can you tell me why the stars shine in the sky?"

"Yes, they—"

"No, you cannot." She stomped her foot. "You might know why they shine, but you don't know how they came to be where they are, or what lies beyond them. But they still exist."

She moved closer to him and continued her diatribe. "What about gravity? Aristotle thought he understood it. You don't fully understand it either, but it exists." She placed her hands on his cheeks and forced him to look at her. "There are infinitely more unanswered questions than there are answers. You don't have to prove something to feel it, to know it exists."

She stepped back. "Don't you see it yet? You. Are. In. Love. With Abigail."

"No, I'm…" Good heavens, she was correct. Though he couldn't prove it with science or math, it was there, in his heart, in his soul. Maybe she didn't return his love, but he had to find out for sure before it was too late.

Georgiana grinned. "What are you going to do about it?"

"I'm going to need your assistance. You better have Henrietta summoned."

Chapter Twenty One

It had gone on long enough. She had let her engagement to Edmund continue for far too long. As much as she dreaded severing her ties with him, it was time for her to publicly cry off and release him from any obligation to her. Abigail attempted to focus on *Cinderella*, but she kept coming back to the fact that Edmund was her prince and she was pushing him away. Of course, Cinderella hadn't trapped her prince. He actually wanted to marry her.

The front door opened and she left the settee to peek out the window. There was no horse or carriage in front of the house, so it must have been someone on foot. She sat back down and picked up her sketch book. Though it was difficult to keep her focus, she had made some progress with a new design, which was fortunate since she had decided that in absence of a family of her own, she would attempt to occupy herself designing gowns.

"I can show myself in." Georgiana's voice carried from

the corridor.

Abigail rose to greet her.

"You must pack immediately."

She froze. "What's wrong?"

Georgiana grabbed Abigail's hands and towed her back to the settee. "I am abducting you. Well, Hen and I are abducting you. We're taking you to Townsend Manor."

"Georgiana, what are you suggesting? I don't understand."

She sighed. "I badgered Edmund into admitting that you were going to cry off, so we decided it would be best for you to come with us to the country, and Edmund will remain in town to announce that it was an amicable break and so forth."

"Georgiana, I cannot run away. And it isn't fair to leave Edmund here to weather the storm alone."

"Nonsense. He will be fine. It has already been arranged and you are coming."

A shuffling noise in the corridor caught her attention and she glanced up to spot her trunk being carried by two footmen.

Abigail leapt up. "What in the world?"

Georgiana grabbed her hand and stopped her forward momentum. "We've already made the arrangements with your father and Judith."

"But…when? How?"

Georgiana pulled on her hand. "Come along now. Hen is waiting for us in the carriage."

• • •

Abigail awoke as the carriage slowed. She hadn't expected

to fall asleep, but several weeks of restless nights had piled up until she was near to exhaustion. They came to a halt and she glanced out upon a cottage.

"Where are we?" she asked.

"We are at Townsend Manor." Henrietta glanced at her sister. "We thought you might enjoy having your own place to stay."

"My own place?"

"Yes, so you can catch up on your rest and perhaps work on some of your sketches, or read your fairy tale books. Whatever you want."

Abigail glanced between them.

"You look like a scared goose." Georgiana laughed. "We have a maid assigned to you, and look, the Manor is just over there, in easy walking distance."

Footmen approached and removed her trunk from the back of the carriage. It was a charming little cottage. Perhaps she wouldn't mind having some time to herself. After all, this was what she had to look forward to for the rest of her life. If she was lucky, Papa would provide her with an allowance and allow her to move to her own small home in a few years.

Yet another footman handed her down from the carriage, and she stretched and walked along the flower beds, admiring the crocus and daffodils.

"We'll see you up at the house for tea. Go and get yourself settled in." Georgiana waved as the carriage moved off toward the big house.

Abigail entered the open door of the cottage and closed it softly behind her. Though it was small, the interior was quite sumptuous. The modest dining room held a rich mahogany table, which conjured unwanted thoughts of Edmund as his hair was precisely the color of the table. Before she could explore further, the door from the kitchen opened and a maid came through.

"My lady." She curtsied. "I am Rachel. I will be taking care of you while you're here. I must away to the big house to gather a few necessities, but I will return shortly."

"Thank you, Rachel." She watched as the maid exited through a side door, then she went to explore the rest of the house. The parlor held two chairs and a lavish, oversized chaise longue covered with a luxurious blue silk fabric and had an entire wall of bookshelves filled with what appeared to be brand new books. She stepped closer and read a few of the titles. There was a copy of Charles Perrault's *The Tales of Mother Goose*. After running her hand gently down the leather-bound spine, she picked up the book and opened it. It was an original that had been hand copied and drawn. Carefully sliding it back in its place on the shelf, she continued perusing the books and soon found an edition of Madame d'Aulnoy's *Les Contes des Fées* that was identical to her own. It seemed almost as if this room had been designed especially for her. A shiver slid down her spine when she discovered the Grimm Brothers' *Children's and Household Tales*. Carefully removing it from the shelf, she turned toward the chaise longue and stifled a scream when she realized the man who stood in the doorway was Edmund.

Her heart threatened to cease beating altogether. "Wh— what are you doing here? I was told you were in London."

He gestured toward the book. "I see you found the new edition of *Children's and Household Tales*."

"You…you bought all of these books for me?" she asked as understanding dawned. "How did you know I was waiting for this book?" she whispered, feeling as if she might shatter at any moment.

"You spoke of it with Lord Oakley in your parlor."

How could he have taken note of that, or even have remembered it? "But Mr. Cross promised to give me the first copy."

Edmund took a step toward her, and she resisted her instinct to take a step back. "I am very difficult to dissuade when there is something I am determined to have."

Suddenly Abigail was no longer sure they were talking about the book. She swallowed. He took another step toward her and a jolt of awareness shot through her.

"Abigail, there is no cause for you to be afraid of me."

"I don't fear you. It's my feelings for you that I fear."

He closed the distance between them instantly and took her into his arms. "Does that mean you've changed your mind about wanting to marry me?"

She shook her head. "No. There was never a time I didn't want to marry you."

He pulled back and looked into her eyes. "Then why did you say those words to me?"

She sucked in a shuddering breath. "Because you deserve more. You deserve better than to be trapped into a marriage against your will."

"Darling, I told you before, I rarely let anyone force me to do something I don't want to do." He took her hands and led her to the settee, then sat and pulled her down next to him. Her heart nearly skipped a beat, then surged into action so quickly she couldn't catch her breath.

"I have been working for weeks to devise a formula to prove that love exists. Though I was certain it wasn't possible, and therefore that romantic love did not exist, I have proven myself wrong."

He knelt in front of her. "The formula was deceptively simple." He pulled a pin from her hair. "Much like these hair pins. Such a rudimental design, and yet they perform their intended purpose with ease." He continued to remove the pins from her hair, smoothing each strand as he released it.

When he finished, he sat back on his haunches and studied her. "I have had vivid dreams of seeing you like this." He tangled his fingers in her hair. "Shame on my imagination for being so uninspired."

He leaned close and took a deep breath, inhaling the scent of her hair. "Where was I? Oh, yes."

Her breath hitched as he placed his hands on either side of her face, looking into her eyes. "You see, nothing works properly without you. I've been floating through each day, as if gravity has somehow stopped affecting me, or someone has disproven the Pythagorean Theorem."

Abigail had no idea what the Pythagorean Theorem was, but he seemed to be trying to tell her something important. Something that caused hope to ignite within her for the first time in many weeks.

"Our formula for love is as simple as the Pythagorean Theorem. You + me + trust squared = love."

He kissed her then, his lips searing a path straight to her ailing heart.

This wasn't one of her daydreams or fairy tales. He was really here with her. She leaned back on the settee and pulled him on top of her, wanting to show him what she couldn't put into words. His heat and the solidness of him surrounded her, giving her courage. Her hands itched to touch his skin.

He pulled back and she moaned, wanting more. "I want to touch you."

Suddenly embarrassed by her own boldness, she turned away, but he wouldn't allow her to hide. Placing a finger under her chin, he turned her head to meet his eyes. "I am yours. Do with me as you please."

Reaching her shaking fingers to his neck, she untied his cravat and tossed it on the floor. She explored the hollow of his throat with her fingers, then pushed the top of his shirt open to reveal his chest. A muscle flexed as she ran her fingers over his skin, and she reveled in her newfound power.

Suddenly he leapt from the settee, tugged his shirt over his head, and removed his boots, leaving him clad only in his breeches. She sat up and turned her back to him so he could unfasten her gown and stays.

His warm breath caressed the back of her neck before his lips gently explored. He slowly opened her gown and kissed each inch of skin as it was bared. A thrill shot down her spine. He pushed her gown off of her shoulders and turned her to face him, pressing her gently against the back of the settee.

Wanting more from him, she pulled him in for a kiss. When her lips parted for air, he took advantage and explored her mouth with his tongue, sending frissons down to the apex of her thighs. Her lips tingled as he moved downward, kissing his way over her pulse and down to her collar bone, where he dipped his tongue into the hollow. Grasping the edge of her gown, he slowly pulled it down while he lavished a searing path down to her breast.

He pulled back to look at her. "You are exquisite." He

cupped her breast reverently, then slowly took her nipple into his mouth and laved it gently, combusting a fire in her that sent flames down through her abdomen. Her hips sprung up off the settee, showing that she wanted more from him.

He feathered his fingers across her stomach, pushing her heart to an erratic rhythm. She gasped and he pulled back.

"Don't," she said.

"Don't what?"

"Don't stop."

As if by magic, he removed every last bit of her clothing with one swift tug. Her eyes popped open in surprise, and she watched as he pushed his breeches to the floor and stepped out of them. She gulped and closed her eyes.

"Look at me, Abigail." He knelt next to the settee, magnificent in his nakedness. "Will you let me love you?"

She nodded and reached for him, pulling him onto her. He shifted to the side and his warm hand returned to her belly, then his fingers danced lazily down. He trailed a finger down her thigh and she shivered in response. His wickedly sensuous lips trailed a path toward her breast, and she shoved her hands into his hair and drew his head to her. He pulled her nipple into his mouth, sending shockwaves downward. His hand stroked between her legs and his weight atop her was the only thing that kept her tethered to the earth. Then he slid one finger inside her and rubbed her with his thumb. She bit back a scream.

"No, my darling. Do not censor yourself. I want to hear your satisfaction." She released a low moan and was rewarded with faster movement from his thumb, his strokes coming faster and faster until she felt she would ignite. And then she did, rubbing herself wantonly against his hand as fireworks went off inside her. Her skin flushed and beads of perspiration bloomed on her forehead.

He slid up her body, capturing her mouth, their bodies fitting together like missing pieces to a puzzle. Using his fingers first to stretch her opening, he then slid inside and stopped. He distracted her with kisses, then pushed through her barrier with one swift movement. She tensed, then relaxed as his lips left a searing path down her neck. He began to move slowly inside her, rekindling the flames from before, and she slid her hands to his shoulders, encouraging him to move faster. She opened her eyes and met his as she shattered in his arms.

• • •

Edmund stared into her eyes, darkening like a stormy sky as she trembled under him. He held himself in check until it became almost painful, her hot flesh nearly scorching him, and with one final thrust, he welcomed his release.

Rolling onto his side, he pulled her tight against him. "I love you," he said, kissing her eyelids, nose, and finally, her lips. He propped his head on his hand and looked down at her.

"Stop staring at me." She waved a hand toward him. "You're making me nervous."

"I can't. You're so beautiful, and I can't believe you're mine. I don't know what I did to deserve you."

"You're you." She pressed a kiss to his lips. "You might even deserve to be sainted, or to have your own harem for putting up with me and your sisters."

The thought of more women in his life made him cringe. "No, thank you. One woman is more than enough for me. As long as she's you." He kissed her back, then tucked her head under his chin, content simply to hold her.

"Once we return to London, I shall require your assistance in getting some of the women in my life out of my house."

She giggled and he gave her a playful slap on her rump.

"So, how did you manage to orchestrate my abduction?"

"It was surprisingly simple. I simply spoke with your father and told him I thought it was time for us to marry. He agreed. Then I enlisted the aid of Georgiana and Henrietta to get you here. Your parents are set to arrive tomorrow to attend the wedding, and they'll be bringing my mother and the rest of my sisters along. I've already secured a special license."

"My goodness. You've thought of everything."

"In truth, I thought only of you."

She pulled him to her and kissed him hungrily, providing empirical proof of the validity of his formula.

Epilogue

Though neither of them wanted to leave, they had stayed at Townsend Manor long enough. Under his supervision, they had finally finished installing all of the glass panes in the greenhouse. Edmund was needed in London, and if they waited too much longer, travel would be uncomfortable for Abigail.

Though the entire manor was at their disposal, Abigail still favored the tiny parlor in the cottage. Sure enough, he found his wife there, stretched out on the chaise longue, reading one of her favorite stories and clad only in her dressing gown. Baxter thumped his tail against the floor as Edmund approached.

He sat next to her and kissed up her neck, traveling over her chin to capture her mouth. Her hair was loose about her shoulders, and he wasted no time sinking his hands into it. Several minutes later, she began to squirm and he pulled back. "The baby is kicking." She took his hand and slid it inside her dressing gown, pressing it against the left side of her stomach. His mouth curved into a wide grin. Sure enough, he could feel soft movements under her skin. Though she had been feeling it for weeks now, this was his first experience.

He knelt next to the chaise and placed his lips against her stomach. "Hello there."

She ran her fingers through his hair. "That tickles."

"If you think that tickles…" He proceeded to move his lips across her abdomen, kissing, licking, and murmuring adoring words to the baby until Abigail dissolved into giggles.

"Enough." She pulled him up to lay next to her on the chaise. "My bladder control isn't what it used to be and you may end up with an unwelcome surprise if you don't stop."

Suitably chastised, he was content simply to relax with her in his arms. "Darling, we really must head back to London soon."

"Yes, I do believe you are right." She ran her hand across the stubble on his cheek, and he pulled her tighter against him. "I received a letter from Georgiana today."

"Hmmm."

"Don't you want to know what she wrote?" She raised a brow.

"That depends."

"On what?"

"What she wrote."

She smacked his shoulder. "She says that all of the soldiers have now returned from the continent, and there still isn't anyone who has caught her fancy."

"Why am I not surprised?"

"Just wait. She also mentioned one man several times. She finds him 'abrasive and irritating,' and 'insufferably arrogant.'"

He bolted upright. "Does this mean what I think it means?"

"It means that we must return to London immediately, as it seems that Georgiana has met her match."

"Lord help us all."

OTHER BOOKS BY ALLY BROADFIELD

How to Beguile a Duke

Just a Kiss

Acknowledgments

To my extremely patient editor, Robin Haseltine. To Heidi Stryker, production editor extraordinaire, and to everyone else at Entangled who helps transform my manuscripts into books.

To my family, my motivation for everything.

To my readers, for making it so rewarding to be an author.

About the Author

Ally has worked as a horse trainer, director of marketing and development, freelance proofreader, and a children's librarian, among other things. None of them were as awesome as writing romance novels (though the librarian gig came closest). She lives in Texas and is convinced her house is shrinking, possibly because she shares it with three kids, four dogs, a cat, a rabbit, and assorted reptiles. Oh, and her husband.

Ally likes to curse in Russian because very few people know what she's saying, and spends most of what would be her spare time letting dogs in and out of the house and shuttling kids around. She has many stories in her head looking for an opportunity to escape onto paper. She writes historical romance set in Regency England and Imperial Russia.

You can find Ally on her website, Facebook, and Twitter, though she makes no claims of using any of them properly. For information about contests and new releases, join her mailing list.